THE SEDUCTRESS

THE
SEDUCTRESS

LEE CARSON

As told to Con Sellers

CUTTING EDGE

ISBN-13: 978-1-962896-50-4

Published by
Cutting Edge Books
PO Box 8212
Calabasas, CA 91372
www.cuttingedgebooks.com

CHAPTER ONE

M en are peculiar about lying around naked. Give them half a chance, and they'll scramble to put on their shorts. Feeling somehow protected once more, they can stretch sated upon the bed and gloat possessively as they watch a woman move across the room in her bare skin.

Joe had on white shorts with red polka dots. His flat belly was ridged with muscle, his powerful chest matted with thick hair. He was strong and experienced and ambitious. The combination made him quite a lover, but not as good as he thought he was.

I turned from the hotel dresser, holding my too-big handbag across my stomach. The picture must have been incongruous, since I was nude. Joe laughed.

He was still chuckling when I brought my right hand out of the bag. The smile stiffened on his face when he saw the bulky, mishappen muzzle of the .38 pointed at him.

"Lee!" he snapped. "That ain't funny, baby. Who set me up for the gag—Petey? Herman? Okay, they had their laugh. Now put that damned thing down."

Over the bulge of the silencer, I picked a spot. "It's no gag, Joe. No hard feelings, though."

He sat up, paling. I shifted the muzzle.

"What the hell—" he began, but I didn't let him finish. There's no point in prolonging these things.

I shot Joe Quade through the left eye. The gun bucked in my fist, its recoil stronger because of the blowback from the silencer.

It made a noise like somebody sneezing hard. Joe Quade's head slammed back onto the pillow. His bare feet drew up, lifting his knees. They twitched jerkily, then slid back down.

It was a net hit, efficient, unmessy. That's the way I liked a job to go. I didn't have to check the door. It had been locked ever since Joe brought me into the room. Joe was careful that way. Only not careful enough. Few men are.

I put the .38 Positive back into the oversized purse and went into the bath. Under the shower, I soaped my hair vigorously, and stood relaxed under the warm water until the last vestiges of color had washed down the drain.

When I went back into the room, I was a brunette again. I wrapped the silk bandanna around my damp hair and pinned it into place. Without makeup, I looked meek, washed-out, nothing like the flamboyant redhead who'd swivel-hipped into the lobby on Joe Quade's arm.

Dressing, I didn't look over at the body on the bed. I wasn't afraid, or squeamish, or anything like that. That wasn't a man any more; it wasn't the man who had so recently made violent love to me, who had cupped my writhing haunches in his strong hands and lifted the rhythm of my hips to him, who had pillowed his dark head against the fevered cones of my taut and thrusting breasts.

Right now Joe Quade was only a lump of meat, without power to move me one way or another. The bullet-punctured shell on the bed meant only another hit made, another job finished. When the newspapers printed the story, a cautious and anonymous runner would bring an envelope to my place in Palm Springs. In it would be ten thousand tax-free dollars.

Inch by inch, I went over the room with a busy handkerchief, smearing any surfaces that may have held my prints. I'd already wiped the bath fixtures. With a final glance around, I fixed the lock so it would snap behind me, and eased out into the hall. Bypassing the elevator, I went down three flights of stairs, and waited until the desk clerk was busy with incoming guests. Slowly, I crossed the lobby and went into the street, blending with the early evening crowds.

I knew how I looked—like a frowsy and harassed young housewife shopping for a late dinner, or a kid slouching home from the library. I'm small enough to pass for a teen-ager. Nobody would notice, nobody would really see me. Being faceless and unremembered is an important asset in my business.

People drifted past me, and I thought of the pleased smugness on Joe's face when I begged him to meet me early. He thought I couldn't wait to be near him, that I ached for his virile strength and maleness. Maybe I did—a little. But that wasn't the reason I didn't hold off until our usual after-midnight date.

I wanted Joe in the hotel while it was still noisy and busy. Sounds are magnified in the stillness of the small hours, and so are memories.

Nondescript, four years old, the car I used while in Los Angeles was waiting where I'd left it. I got in, slipped the gun into a special clamp under the dash and drove off, heading east on the freeway. An hour and a half down the road, I'd pull into a certain dusty garage with a wrecking yard out back. I'd exchange the old Chevy for a gleaming-white T-Bird. There, I'd also take time for the final protective touch—a melted wax bath for my right hand, just in case. The cops weren't the only ones who knew about the paraffin test. My candlewax did just as well, removing the microscopic particles of gunpowder from the pores of my skin.

The garage owner was a Combine man. He'd dismantle the .38 and see that its component parts were crushed beyond recognition, that the shapeless bits of metal were included in his next shipment of junk. Briefly, I wondered what the melted-down .38

would help make up, next time it was used—a jukebox, baby buggy, a pot for a still?

That would be ironic, if it ended as part of an alky cooking pot. Ironic because that was what had caused a bullet to be slapped into Joe Quade's brain. As I said, Joe was ambitious, and had a yen for more pots than he tallied with the Combine.

But that wasn't my end of the business. I didn't give a damn why a contract was set up for a hit. I just followed through, without questions. Questions are for cops.

After I left the garage, I peeled off the bandanna and let the night wind flow through my hair. There was fresh makeup on my face, and the shoes from my clothes cache had cost fifty dollars. They fitted with the air-conditioned, convertible T-Bird. So did I. I was warmly relaxed, back into the playgirl character of Palm Springs.

And I felt the familiar tingle in my loins, knew a driving excitement building within me. A hit usually affected me this way, stimulating, making the blood pump faster, drying my mouth. I squirmed on the car's leather seat, brushing one thigh against the other, trying to stifle the itch I couldn't scratch. I pushed the gas pedal closer to the floor, exulting in the surge of the car, the stepped-up thunder of its powerful motor.

Watch it, I told myself as off-freeway lights of some desert town whipped by; watch it. I dropped back to the speed limit. It wouldn't matter much if Lee Carson picked up another traffic ticket. There were plenty already on her record. But the incident might forge a tiny link in a chain of suspicion. A lot of people in my business have walked into the little Green Room at San Quentin, because of such tiny links.

Not that the average cop would even dream that the poolside, champagne-sipping, society playgirl might be a professional gun. The idea was too far beyond the average cop's imagination.

Only it wasn't the average cops I had to watch. It was the unaverage ones.

So I stayed at a safe sixty-five miles an hour, babying the T-Bird along over the sweeping stretches of Highway 99, through Beaumont and Banning. After the village of Cabazon, it was only minutes to the turnoff, the twisty route that would bring me to the plush and pampered colony of the rich at Palm Springs.

That was Lee Carson's front, the surroundings she enjoyed. Everybody knew her there, everyone saw her at one or another of the continuing parties that ran practically day and night, the dancing, glass-waving, pool-splashing brawls that passed for entertainment among the elite and grifters alike.

The lights of the town lay ahead, and I slowed the car. I was home free, with a clean and profitable hit behind me, and the tips of my breasts ached to be free of the linen cups that confined them. Soon I could let myself go, soon I could find one of the sunbronzed bodies to ease the building pressure inside me. In just minutes, I could forget that I was known in the high circles of crime as The Widow. It was a name backing a reputation of quick and silent efficiency. It was a name the big boys trusted. Whenever they stopped trusting, it would be engraved on a lonely tombstone, and my small body would be under that polished slab of granite.

That's the way it is, in this business. Louse up one job, let rumors of a payoff get back to the big boys, and a new contract would be made. Only this time, I'd be on the wrong end of the gun.

I slammed the T-Bird to a stop in the carport of the sprawling place I leased out on the edge of town. What the hell was I worrying about? I knew the rules of the game before I started to play, and I hadn't broken any of them yet. I didn't intend to.

The house was faintly musty. I flipped the air-conditioner switch, thumbed the lights and went across the big room to the phone. The call I made was personal, not business. I didn't have to report. Tomorrow's papers would do that for me, after some bellhop or maid discovered the body. The news wouldn't be buried on the obituary page. Joe Quade was too well known.

I listened to the buzzing of the signal at the other end of the line. Wally didn't answer. I let the phone ring a few more times, then dropped it back into its cradle. Wally Metcalf wasn't handy. Okay, I'd find another man. It wouldn't be difficult.

Not as long as I fill out a dress the way I do. I may not be so tall, but everything is where it should be. A lot of men go for very small girls. I have no particular preference, personally. My lovers can be towering or short, wide or slim, young or middle-aged. If they're strong and willing, and don't have a rim of dirt around their necks, that's all I ask. And maybe that they're intelligent enough to experiment.

Wally and the rest of my "friends" didn't know I was back in town. Okay, so I'd go out and scare up a little excitement on my own, find a new and different man to play with.

At least, until the next time my telephone rang, and a rasping voice gave me another name and another contract. Then I'd have to stop playing and go off on another business trip.

But tonight was mind, to do with as I damned well pleased. So I put all five feet, two inches and all ninety-five pounds of me snugly into a clinging, strapless evening gown, and skipped back to my car for a night on the town. I needed gaiety, laughter, fun. I needed companionship. I needed a man.

On nights like this, I just can't stand being alone. I never could, really. But especially on nights after I've made a hit, I have to be with somebody. It seems that even the stars are dark, and that their cold, black shadows will close me in if I'm alone.

CHAPTER TWO

I think I started my story in the middle; or maybe, pretty close to the end. I guess everything will be clearer if I go back to the beginning. Nobody springs full-blown into a business like mine. You have to start somewhere, and something has to push you into it.

I'm not making alibis for myself. The hell with that. I read where some headshrinker says there are no bad kids, only bad parents. It makes me want to spit. I'm no authority on juvenile delinquents, and I sure as hell don't want to be.

But I know this much—I've seen senselessly savage little punks come out of well-to-do, loving families, and don't want a damned thing to do with kids who chop up helpless people for "kicks." They don't last long, anyway. They either run into some guy who's really tough, or the law gets tired of telling them to go and repent, and finally sends them up for a long stretch.

Either way, the delinquent gets it in the neck. Because if some gunman doesn't get them on this side of the bars, time-hardened old cons will get them on the other side. It's kind of pitiful to watch a "tough" kid's ego crumble, when he's made to get down and lick shoes. And worse, a hell of a lot worse. Guys cut off from normal sex lives just wait for a young kid to get sent up.

How do I know? Well, the authorities haven't gotten around to coeducational prisons yet, but from what I've seen on the inside of women's pens, and from what I've heard about the others, there isn't much difference. Sure I did a fall once. Damned near everybody on the wrong side of the law does.

But the smart ones learn something. The not-so-smart ones go back, for one stretch after another, until, all of a sudden they're old and they wonder where all the years went; I'm not exactly stupid, so my first fall was my last. If I'm ever picked up again, I'll wind up breathing cyanide fumes in the gas room.

If I ever make it to death row, that is. There are some people who might not like the idea of me pining away and thinking hard in prison. Those people could get the idea that I'm getting old and soft and scared. Scared people make deals. Scared people spill their guts to the cops. So it figures that I'd never make it. They'd find a way to shut me up, quick.

Hell, I'm getting ahead of myself in one way, and behind in another. If I'm going to make any sense out of this, I'd better try to get my story organized. But before I go into the whys and hows of my life, you might as well know that all the names you'll see are phony, even my own.

And I've changed a lot of times, places and backgrounds, so nobody can pinpoint the events. There's a damned good reason for doing this. I want to keep living for awhile.

Some of you may think this is a lot of jazz, that I'm making everything more dramatic than it really is. I can just hear some of you now: "Well, I suppose this is all right—as fiction. But of course, nothing like that has gone on in this country since the 20's, since the Capone and bootlegging days."

Yeah? If you think the Combine is fiction, if you think hired guns are a thing of the past, you'd better crawl out of your shell and start looking around. Remember a man called Buggsy Seigel? Remember a few years back, when some "person or persons unknown" stuck an automatic carbine through the window of Buggsy's plush California living room and blew hell out of him?

While we're about it, you might recall Albert Anastasia, stretched out in a barber chair, right in the middle of New York. "Persons unknown" put pistols to Al's head and blasted away. The barqers developed lockjaw.

How about Roger "The Terrible" Touhey? How long was he out of jail before "unknown" gunners cut him down on his front steps? It seems to me that hit came off only last year. What's the score on the bootlegging era now?

Maybe you'll notice one thing those hits had in common. All were committed by "person or persons unknown." Funny, isn't it? Some sex-sick doctor and his mistress can knock off the doc's wife, and bing! The cops have them. A psychotic janitor can run amok with a furnace stoker and kill two or three women, and bing! The cuffs are on him. A wife can poison her husband—bing! She's on death row.

But the gangland hits, the real professional jobs, how about them? The years pass, and the gunners are still not fingered. They still remain "persons unknown." There are two main reasons for this. One—protection; two—the gunners were pros. The hits were unemotional, planned and carried out in a businesslike manner by contract guns that came into town, made the hits and left. The Combine never uses local talent. Imported guns are much safer. They're not recognized, they have no connection with the target, they don't stick around, the payoff isn't spent in local joints.

Yeah, and there's another fallacy you may as well clear out of your thinking—that the bootlegging era is a thing of the past. Listen, bootlegging is the life blood of the Combine. Sure, it dabbles in dope and women and gambling, but those sidelines are only the butter for the bread. Bootlegging is the bread itself.

You wonder how such an operation can be profitable since the prohibition laws were repealed? You classify bootlegging with some bearded character outrunning revenuers in the comic strips? You've got a lot to learn, mister, and I guess this is a good place for your first lesson.

Prohibition was before my time, but several of the guys who hire me got their start about then. They also got some very bright ideas about booze and the great American public. The smart boys didn't retire just because the Feds wised up and said okay, everybody can drink legally now.

The smart boys took a close look at what the government was doing with whiskey taxes, and decided that those taxes would keep right on climbing in the future. And they were right. They kept the stills in operation, slowly at first, and a hell of a lot cleaner and more efficient than in the hectic turn-it-out days.

The Feds figured on maybe a billion dollars in taxes, and when they didn't get all they expected, they yelled to raise the taxes more. The legit distillers tried to point out that if taxes go up, so does the cost of booze, and when booze costs more, there are less sales, and therefore less tax money coming in. But the socialistic, welfare-staters in the Revenue department never listened. They just kept their hands out.

Nobody listened—except the bootleggers. They heard and applauded. Do you have any idea what the tax-per-gallon rate is now? Ten dollars and fifty cents, and there's no sign that it won't keep rising.

Now try to picture a concern that turns out fifty to a hundred million gallons of 190 proof alcohol every year. This stuff—clean and potent as any in the world—is peddled to distributors for maybe $2.50 a quart. The profit is around one thousand percent, over and above protection money and operating costs.

A big man in the illegal liquor racket explained it to me this way: the stuff costs him around $1.92 per gallon to produce raw. Some of it he sold to juice joints where it would be cut three or four ways with water and still bring forty cents a shot. That averages to something like $270 on a five gallon can. But my friend had other angles going for him too. He had legit bottles of top brands and peddled the homemade booze under any name in demand—labels, tax stamps and everything

It's big business—so damned big that the Combine feeds from it. And remember that the Combine is only one organization. There are others just as big, just as rich. The territory lines are sharply drawn, though, and any time one of the local boys gets a shade too ambitious and tries to expand, somebody will sigh and pick up a phone. They'll call a guy in Detroit, or New Orleans or Tacoma or San Diego, and give a name and price.

Or they'll call me, The Widow.

Okay, the first lesson is over. Maybe you've learned that bootlegging still buys goldplated Cadillacs and diamond-studded yachts, and maybe you believe the Combine is as real and harsh as a .38 caliber slug. So I guess it's time for lesson two.

Shielded by your sick, insecure egos, you men find it hard to believe that a mere woman, and a tiny one at that, can snuff out a human life with the same unemotional deftness a man uses. I'm glad you think that way. I'm glad I look soft and sexy and not strong enough for anything except a roll in the hay. It's a hell of a lot easier for me to get close to a nervous and suspicious target.

The Combine realizes that, now. It took some convincing, at first, but now I'm accepted as one of the best in the profession. I get as many calls as any hairy-chested gunner, and my bank account will prove it.

School's out for awhile. I'll try to get on with what I started to do—giving you the story of my life. I don't know why. Maybe I feel that I want to leave more behind me than just a tombstone eroding in the wind. Perhaps there's a need for confession in me now; I'm not sure. Hell, I might just have a long-dormant creative drive. Wouldn't that be a laugh? I mean, if I could have been a writer all these years, instead of what I am?

But nobody will be able to make sense out of this story if I don't stop wandering all over the place. Okay, so we'll go back as they do in the movies, and fill the customer in on the early years of the star.

In Shuba, Mississippi, I didn't feel like a star. I didn't feel like much of anything, I guess. Not when I grew up enough to realize a little of what was going on around me. I remember being jumpy most of the time, jittery as a swamp rabbit when he hears the hounds. I remember dreading Saturdays, because that's when I had to go the nine miles through the piney woods into Shuba with the family to do our shopping.

The family. That's a laugh. The only real family I had was Ma, and she was only a sick and whining shadow, somehow already dead. I didn't count Jett and Pete Finney as family. They came along after Pa died. Jett married Ma, and brought his son Pete along to live with us.

I think of Jett and Pete, and I get so damned mad it makes me sick at my stomach. And the sickness carries over to other names in the two-bit town of Shuba, and still farther, to others in the county seat.

But if I'm objective about it, I see where I ought to thank Jett and his leering, redneck son for chasing me off the poor-dirt farm and out of the state itself. If I hadn't run, I'd be the spitting image of Ma by now—tired, spiritless, worked to the bone and stupid. And tied to some lazy, worthless backwoods trash just like Jett Finney.

The hard-dirt section of Mississippi is hell on women, and maybe hell on the right kind of men, too. It's starvation-poor, bug-ridden and miserable. Most folks don't know enough to get out, don't know any better than to work from can't-see to can't-see, just trying to get by on a patch of land whose strength was burned out long ago.

Then there are the others, the white trash who hole up in the piney woods, scratching a few shrunken vegetables out of the ground, feeding off a few scrawny chickens and the woods, standing hat in hand to beg credit from the Shuba storekeepers. Credit for tobacco and a bag of flour and maybe some lard and salt.

Hell, it still goes on today. I know, because I went back a few years ago, just to see. And to do something that needed doing for a long time. But I'll get to that part later. Right now I'm trying to remember how I must have looked then. I was little and sunbrowned and skinny. I always had a dull ache in my belly, because three seasons out of the year, I was hungry. In Spring, the woods were full of blackberries and mayhaws and wild onions; the creeks teemed with sunperch and channel cats; the trees were full of squirrels and the canebrakes noisy with rabbits.

Nobody paid any attention to hunting licenses or regulations. We trapped and shot and caught what we could, whenever we could. I guess "we" is just a figure of speech, because Lee Green was always alone. That was my name then—Green. The guy I married later was named Carson. Other names would have fit him better—grifter, blackmailer, pimp. But I'm wandering again. Don Carson wasn't part of my life then.

What the hell was? Pine trees and water oaks and brown creek water. And Monday washings with lye soap in a big, smokeblack iron pot, stirring the threadbare overalls and denim shirts with a bleached oak paddle, using the same flat stick to pound the heavy clothes clean.

What else? Chopping stovewood because Jett and Pete were lying drunk at the still back off by the creek. Swinging a hoe at weeds that were choking off the rows of summer corn and squash and turnips. Lying awake on a cornshuck mattress and listening to the rats scamper in the loft over my head. Lying awake to hear Ma's thin, whining protests and the rusted rattle of bedsprings as Jett grunted and snorted his way to satisfaction. Learning to watch for signs that would tell me just how drunk Jett and Pete were, because when they'd passed a certain, sourstink point, I'd have to slip out of the shack and run for the woods.

Moccasins in the pinestraw, slithering across the mud banks, lying slim and deadly beneath the crabapple trees; cottonmouth and copperhead and the thick-bodied water moccasins. I learned to respect the snakes; they never tried to get me unless I stepped too close. They didn't start trouble.

Jett Finney did. Whenever Ma's back was turned, he'd be pinching and patting, and putting himself up to my skirt by accident. But Jett was old and slow, and I could stay away from him pretty good. It was Pete I had to watch close. He was young—two years older than me—and he was strong. Sneaky, too.

Like the time he creeped back of the henhouse and grabbed. I didn't know he was anywhere near the house. I jumped and damned near dropped the hoe I was holding. He had his whole damned hand—

I wheeled away, or tried to. Pete whinnied and snatched a handful of my hair. It was long then, down to my hips, and it made a pretty good grip to hold me by. I gritted my teeth against the pain and swung the hoe handle. Its length landed just where I wanted it to—in his crotch.

I didn't hit him hard enough. He turned white as a flour sack and jerked himself into a knot, but he still had the strength to dodge when I reversed the hoe and chopped at his head with the flat blade. He ran off doubled-over, cursing back at me.

That's how it was, for nearly two years—me keeping one eye on Pete Finney, and the other on his Pa. Between times, I didn't have much time to notice how Ma was fading away, becoming more stooped, more silent and wraithlike. But then, I didn't stay around the house much. It was safer and cleaner in the woods, where I could make up dreams of places and people outside the world I knew.

I stole the rifle about then. All Pa had left was an old shotgun, and 20 gauge shells cost too much. But I could swap the colored folks possums for a box of 22's, and I didn't waste them either. Jett Finney's 22 Savage was clip-fed, and it always three a mite to the left. The windage knob was broken, too, but I didn't get many shots over fifty yards away. With the men drunk or running fresh mash through the still, or off peddling their rotgut and whoring among the mulatto girls, it was up to me to put meat on the table for Ma and myself. You can get pretty good with a gun, when you're shooting to fill your belly.

Maybe that's something else I should be grateful to the Finneys for—my know-how with a gun, the ability to hit anything I aim at. Not that I'm an Annie Oakley. I can't take the eye out of a running squirrel at sixty paces. But in my business, most of the work is done close in. It's only once in awhile that I have to use anything but a handgun, and then I can usually take my time, and use the best telescopic sights.

To get back to the way things were building up at the farm—Ma took to bed, and since Jett wouldn't send for the doctor, I went for him myself. Old Doc Wiley took one look at the shack, squinted up at the holes in its shingle roof, and told Jett that Ma was working herself to death. Jett only grunted, and stuck his snout back into the Mason jar full of corn liquor. Doc Wiley gave me some pills for Ma and went back home. It was all he could do.

I got to thinking of what would happen when she died, and I didn't like the picture. I wasn't a damned bit wrong either.

Ma died on Friday morning, and was buried in a raw pine box the same day. Saturday night, her husband and my stepbrother trapped me in the house, while I was getting together the few ragged clothes I owned. I remember the first thing I thought, when I saw them hemming me away from the door, when I made out the whiskey-shine on their faces and saw the red glints in their eyes.

I thought what a damned fool I was, for leaving the rifle hidden out back of the henhouse.

CHAPTER THREE

Balanced on the balls of my bare feet, I looked for a way out. If I went for the door, Pete Finney was in the way, and Jett Finney hemmed me away from the window. They were mean drunk, and I knew I wouldn't be able to claw and knee my way out this time. They meant business, and their business was me.

I tried talking. "Ma—"

"Can't help you now," Pete leered. "Can't nobody help you now. Go ahead—scream; holler your fool head off. I ain't forgot what you done to me with that hoe handle."

"Jett" I said, watching them inch closer, "I'm your step-daughter. It's not right."

His mouth was slack and wet. "You a gal," he mumbled. "Just a gal all prime. You gonna' enjoy it, Lee. It ain't nothin' to be feared of."

I bent low and darted for the kitchen stove. Catching up the handle of one of the clothes irons that say on the old woodburner, I swung the heavy metal in a threatening arc.

"I'll bust you," I said. "I swear I'll bust the first one puts his hands on me."

Jett had his arms spread wide. "Pete," he said, "kick her feet out from under her."

Pete skipped around me, feinting a kick, his flat eyes gleaming, yellow teeth bared in a hungry grin. I made a mistake. I jumped straight at him. I wanted to pound his skull to pieces. I wanted to break his head with the iron.

Jett had me from behind. The thick acrid smell of his sweat clotted my nostrils. The stiff bristles on his face ground into my jaw. One corded arm was under my chin, forcing my head back. The other hand clamped around my wrist. He swung the iron hard against the stove, and my fingers lost their grip on the handle.

I tried to butt backwards. I tried to kick up backwards. His thighs clamped down on my leg. I felt him against me, rubbing into me. The arm across my throat was cutting off air, and I tore at it with both hands.

Pete hit me then. It didn't hurt right away; it just made the oil lamp flash on and off and drained all the strength out of my knees. I fought to move, and couldn't. My body felt like a sack of corn looks, weak and flattening itself when the grain pours out of a torn corner.

I knew they had their hands on me. Fingers squeezed into both my breasts. Fingers twisted at my belly. The room whirled, and I felt the bed against my back, felt my ankles twisted apart and held wide. My thin dress was ripped away from my body, my underclothes torn apart.

I shook my head, trying to clear it. My arms were pulled back over my head, held by the wrists. The position arched my naked breasts for the wet and mewling caress of unshaven lips. I struggled, swinging my hips, tugging at my arms.

They had me. Pete kneeled on one of my legs, held the other with his hands. Jett kept my arms pinned. They had me. There was no way out. I wouldn't cry. Damned if I'd cry and give them that much more satisfaction. I shut my eyes, hearing Pete grunt as he worked at his overalls, hearing the excited rasping of Jett's breath as he watched. My flesh crawled flinching away from the thrust of other flesh. There was a bitter taste in my mouth. My teeth ached from locking them so tightly.

The sons of bitches. Pete crawled all hairy and naked in between my knees, scrunching up between the thighs I couldn't keep shut anymore. He had his thing in his free hand, that big, ugly rod all shiny on the head and drippy. I didn't want it in me, inside me; I swear I didn't.

He sort of hunched over and tried to force it in me, but it wouldn't go right away, so he used his hard, dirty fingers instead. He shoved a finger into my organ, pried the lips apart and worked it hurting inside until I wanted to scream. But I didn't. I wouldn't scream for the bastards; they couldn't make me do that.

Pete worked his finger in and out, then jammed another finger in beside the first one, and I felt something give, felt a hot dampness that made me think I was going to bleed to death. Pete laughed, and Jett cackled with him, and I felt the spongy head of his thing against me down there again, felt it pushing hard into the dampness and the pubic hair, and I hated the pair of them like I've never hated anything else in my life.

He was pushing inside me. His ugly, rigid rod slipped into my vagina inch by hurtful inch, and he took hold of my buttocks to roll me back on my shoulders so he could put it to me all the way deep. His rod went on in, until I thought it was going to split me open. Pete grunted and wiggled some, then began to move back and forth in me, to pump in and out with a squirming motion that I couldn't resist.

Jett held my hands locked, and I knew if I tried to bite Pete that I'd get my jaw broken or maybe an eye gouged out. They didn't care, those two bastards; all they wanted was to screw me until they fell out, and come hell or high water, they were going to do it.

Pete buried it to the hilt in me; he shoved and tugged, and panted as he stroked it in and out, in and out, and I felt something else—a strange, tingly kind of sensation that started in my vagina and was spreading all over the lower part of my body. Pete slammed away at me, packing that thing deep and then pulling it almost all the way back out, and this weird sensation spread wider and deeper inside me. I didn't understand it, couldn't know what it was.

"At's the gal," Pete gasped. "Look at her take it, Pa; look how she enjoys it. Told you she was a good screw; told you!"

I tried to stop squirming, to stop wiggling, but it was like some other woman was inside my skin, and this other woman was purely hot, burning up, needing that thing rammed deeper and harder and longer into her pulsing organ.

"Stick her, boy, stick her!" Jett was leaning over me, trying to see down to where his son was putting it to me, trying to watch every stroke as Pete screwed me. But he never let go my hands, because I kept trying to get them loose—but not to hit anybody. I hated myself for it, but I knew damned well I wanted to wrap my arms around Pete's dirty neck, to pull his gasping mouth down to the nipples of my aching breasts. I wanted to hug the grunting son-of-a-bitch.

Then Pete gave a big, trembling hunch and I felt something else inside my vagina—a spurting, a throbbing, and I realized the bastard had gone off inside me, that he'd pumped his rotten seed deeply into me. But overlapping my disgust was this alien wanting, this strange urgency, and I felt the heat rock me, felt the shaking start behind my knees and spread racing up to my thighs and into my lower belly.

I came then for the first time in my life. I reached a dizzy orgasm with a man I despised, because I was raped by a man who needed killing if anybody ever did.

He stayed there for a long, weakened minute, held his rod inside me and his hairy, swollen sac up against my vulva. I was limp, sick, helpless. I kind of flowed down as he backed off and let my rear touch the floor again. Then Pete took it out of me, pulled it out and grinned down at me as if he'd accomplished something magnificent.

"Liked it, didn't you? Tol' you you'd like it, you little bitch. You got too sweet an ass not to like bein' screwed. Tight and hot, and that's purely how a man likes it."

"Hurry up," his Pa grunted. "Take her hands while she's wore down some. Hold her for me, Pete—hold her so I can put another prick in her afore she slacks off any."

The old man was naked, too, and hairy as any old grey hog. His rod was some shorter than Pete's, but it seemed bigger around. I didn't even try to fight him, or try to struggle with Pete. Once you get wallowed in a mudhole, a little more mud don't make you any dirtier.

Jett shoved it inside me without even petting me. He guided it into the cleft with one hand, giving a series of wiggles and pushes until it slid on up inside me. I was wetter and opened some, so he didn't hurt me like Pete had. Snorting and heaving, the old man stuck it to me, and pretty soon his mouth went down to my breast. He sucked a nipple into his teeth and chewed lightly on it for awhile, and all the time he was pumping back and forth into me for all he was worth, both his hands gripping the cheeks of my buttocks and spreading me wider for his pleasure.

Maybe some psychiatrist can work out why I could lie there and hate him, but still get the good feeling as he laid me. Maybe some smart headshrinker can say why I can both hate and love physically at the same time. I don't know, and I've long since stopped giving much of a damn. But right then it seemed horrible to me that I should shake my rear and hunch my pelvis for the obscene thrustings of the old man, terrible that I worked my vagina over and around that stroking rod so I could enjoy his screwing more. But I did those things, and more. I held his head to my breast after Pete let go my wrists, and I wrapped my legs across his grey hairy back, and I tried to lift him clean through the roof as I screwed him stroke for stroke.

He came, heaving and bucking, and I held him tightly while I laid it harder and faster into him, onto him, so I could hit my own quivering orgasm before he might pull out of me. I wouldn't even let him go after I did reach a climax, but clung panting to him, rolling my hips and arching my back and trying to squeeze his thing deeper into my body by the power of my legs.

"Ain't she a bearcat, tho?" The old man was grinning and trying to untangle himself. "Thought butter wouldn't melt in her mouth; thought her ass was cake and somebody might break the icing. And here so go—stick it to me, stick it to me."

"Hurry up, Pa," Pete whined. "I ain't half done with the bitch yet. Get up off her and I'll pull her up on her knees like this—"

I was still somebody else, some scarlet woman who'd lay any-thing stuck at her, and enjoy it. They balanced me on my knees with my hands hung limp at my sides, and Jett went around in back to sit down tight against my rear and be ready to hold me in case I fought. I had no idea what was going to happen next. I knew about animals and how they did it. Any hard-dirt girl or boy knows that, from seeing it every day around the farm. But farm animals don't do what Pete and Jett wanted to do to me next.

Pete took me by the head and stepped up close in front of me. I stared dully at his thing, all swollen and red, all ready to go once more. It was right up to me, and I saw the wrinkles in the sac, the curling of the hair, the veins standing out in the shaft of the rod.

"Here," he said, "Open up your damned mouth and take this here meat in it. Do what comes naturally, you mealy-mouthed little bitch. Take this here rod in and comfort it, like."

I came awake when he pushed it at me. I pulled back and shook my head, but he held tightly to my hair and tried to put it between my lips. I wouldn't do that. Not with him and not with Jett, and maybe not with any son-of-a-bitch in the whole wide, entire world. But Jett grabbed my arms from behind, and Pete tugged my face closer and I felt the warm touch of it against my tightly shut lips.

Pete rubbed it over my face, ground himself into my face, and I didn't dare open my mouth to scream at him, to curse him for what he was, because if I did, he'd have the chance to slip it in. No, I thought wildly, no, no, no!

The room whirled and I think Pete kicked me in the belly. The breath whooshed! out of me and I tasted something I didn't want to know, and they held me so damned tight, so damned helpless—

Bam—bam—bam.

Everything stopped. Everything stayed just where it was, caught and held motionless by the rapping of knuckles on wood.

I screamed then, screamed so hard and so loud that it strained my throat—screamed before Jett could switch grips and cover my mouth.

"Hey!" the voice said.

There was somebody on the porch, a man at the door. Somebody looking to buy a quart of Jett's rotgut, probably. Nobody else ever came to see us. But it threw Jett and Pete off, surprised them, made them forget me for just a split second.

That was all I needed. Jerking my hands free, I rolled for the edge of the bed as Pete cursed and swung a knotted fist down at me. He missed, and I was on the floor, rolling, yelling for help.

When the door flew open, I was on my feet, pressed against the wall. I must have been a sight, naked from head to foot, wide-eyed and shaking. The stranger stood in the door, staring. "What you doing to that girl?"

Pete cursed him savagely, hissing the words across the lamp-lit room. The man paid no attention. He hadn't stopped looking at me. I put one hand down low on my stomach, spread the other across my breasts. They couldn't cover much.

"T—they're raping me," I said. "They want to put it in my mouth."

Jett moved forward. "No such thing. The gal's kind of sick. My own step-daughter, too. She got sick in the head when her Ma died. We was—we was just tryin' to make her put some clothes on."

The man wasn't from Shuba. He had on a suit and a white shirt, and the lamplight reflected from his pointy shoes. He even had a straw hat. He kept staring at me.

"Help me," I said. "Please help me."

Pete was sliding over to the fireplace. Jett said something else about how crazy I was, more about trying to take care of his poor little step-daughter. The man's eyes were hot on my nude body.

"Folks said I could get some corn whisky here," he said. "Good thing I come when I did."

Pete turned from the mantel piece with the long 20-gauge shotgun in his hands. "Git! Git on outa' here, mister, afore you git more'n you come for."

For the first time, the man looked away from me. He put a hand in his coat pocket. "You keep a loaded shotgun in the house?" he said to Pete.

Pete hesitated, then glanced quickly down as he broke the barrel to see if there was a shell in it. When he looked back up, the stranger had a little shiny pistol in his hand, and he had it pointed right between Pete's eyes.

"Shoot him!" I yelled.

I could hear Jett easing back toward the bed, getting out of range.

"Keep that muzzle pointed at the floor," the man said. "Get some clothes, girl. I'll take you out of here."

Spittle gathered in the corners of Pete's whiskered mouth as he cursed the man, but he didn't lift the shotgun. I moved away from the wall and stepped around Jett.

"Don't let him shoot us, daughter," Jett whined. "We're your folks. Tell him to be careful with that pistol."

I shoved him down on the bed and grabbed at my open cardboard suitcase. Throwing a dress over my head, I started wiggling into it. The dress came down and the man was staring hard at me again, forgetting Pete and the shotgun, forgetting everything but what he could see.

"Look out!" I screamed, but it was too late.

The barrel of the old 20-gauge caught the stranger alongside the head. His pistol skittered across the floor and stopped at my foot. Jett snatched down for it, but I stomped his hand. He scuttled back and jerked a slat out of the bed.

The stranger was on his knees, his eyebrow cut open and blood running down his face. Pete had the stock of the shotgun drawn back for another blow. Jett got in his way when he jumped over and chopped down at the man's head with the bed slat. They were all yelling and grabbing at each other in a tangle of legs and arms.

I stooped for the little pistol. It felt good in my sweaty hand, smooth and firm and balanced. It was the first hand gun I'd ever touched, but I knew what to do with it. Remembering, I guess it was only a .32, a cheap and tiny piston you can pick up in any pawn shop. But it sounded like the crack of doom when I fired it into the wall just over their bobbing heads. It sounded fine.

Faces snapped around at me, white and afraid. Automatically, my thumb eared the gum hammer back for another shot. The cylinder clicked over and put another cartridge under the striker.

"Roll out of the way, stranger," I said. "Pete Finney, throw that gun down—quick!"

One of them did as I said. The stranger rolled away. I remember he rolled over his straw hat and crushed it. Pete didn't listen, and I was glad he didn't. When he tried to point the shotgun at me, that gave me an additional excuse to shoot him. The pistol bucked and spouted noise. The bullet slapped through Pete's left kneecap and knocked his leg out from under him. His shoulder thumped into the floor as he fell. The shotgun bounced out of his hands. I put one foot on it and turned toward Jett.

"No!" he gibbered, and let the bed slat drop. "No, d—daughter—you wouldn't! You wouldn't shoot me!"

"Wouldn't I? You rotten, stinking old man, why the hell do you think I wouldn't? The stranger was rising shakily to his feet. Pete Finney whimpered on the floor, both hands wrapped around his bleeding knee. Coldly, I centered the pistol muzzle on Jett. "Run," I said. "Run, damn you—or I'll kill you where you stand."

Jett's reddened eyes fixed on mine. He saw I meant every word I said. His work shoes scuffed the floor as he tried to outfox me by not going for the door. Awkwardly, crossed arms shielding his face, Jett leaned forward and ran through the window. For a moment, his clumsy body was outlined against the shattering glass and splintering frame. A moment was enough.

He screamed as the bullet hammered through his scrawny tail, and the sound was cut off suddenly when he landed on the hard-packed earth beneath the window. I knew he wasn't dead because I hadn't tried to kill him. I just wanted to tear him up some.

I lowered the smoking gun and looked at the stranger. "You got a car? I didn't hear you drive up."

He rubbed a shaking hand across his face. "Uh—yeah, yeah I got a car. Left it at the road. Didn't want to get stuck in the dark."

"You still want to take me out of here?"

He dabbed at his cut eyebrow with a handkerchief. "Sure, sure, only what about them? You think the old man will live?"

"He'll live," I said. "Jet Finney is too poison mean to die. And so is his whelp there. I'll go with you if you want. Anywhere you say, mister. You put yourself out to help me. I'll do my best to pay you back."

"Yeah," he muttered, "yeah. Look, Miss—"

"Green; Lee Green."

"Pleased to meetcha'. My name is Don Carson, United Farm Equipment. Look, Miss Green, don't you suppose we better do somethin' about these men? I mean, they could die if we don't—"

"Let them," I said. "You, Pete. You better stop that squalling before I get tired of it."

Pete shut up. His daddy was groaning out in the dark.

"Here's my suitcase," I said. "I'll hold onto the pistol until we're down the road apiece. Come on, Don Carson, let's get the hell out of here."

I held Don's hand to guide him over the redclay ruts of the wagon track that led away from the shack. A light wind stirred the sighing tops of secondgrowth pines; the sky was clear and stars were bright. There was a bubbling in my throat, a heady sense of freedom flowing up from inside me.

Don was puffing when we reached the county road. He opened the car door and tossed my suitcase into the back seat. "Jump in. We better hurry. I'd just as soon be away from here before the law finds out."

I slid in beside him. I'd been carrying my only pair of shoes. Now I leaned over and worled the mail order sandals onto my dusty feet. Straightening up as Don flicked on the car lights and gunned the motor, I though of what I would do. I didn't have a dime. There were only three worn and patched dresses in the cheap suitcase, and extra pair of homemade panties and my toothbrush and comb.

But I'd make out. I'd get a job—any kind of job. I was strong, in spite of being so small. I could pull my weight in a hamburger stand, or a filling station, or anywhere. I'd get out of Shuba and Clarkston County as fast as I could.

"Don't worry about the law," I said to the face outlined by the dashlight. "I don't reckon Jett and Pete will say anything. They'll get one of them mulatto girls to bind them up, and they'll just lay drunk until they heal, lickin' their wounds like redbone hounds."

"Damn," Don said. "A fella' just stops in for a quart of stumpjuice, and runs into a real mess. If I hadn't been out to the Johnson place about a broke-down hay rake—"

"You sorry?" I asked. "You looked like an angel to me, mister."

He glanced quickly at me. "No, I guess I'm not sorry. I never seen a girl put together the way you are, Lee Green. Standin' naked in the light like that, why—you make a man's eyes hurt."

My face was hot. I was glad he couldn't see it.

Don kept tailing, and pulled the car off to one side at the traffic light that keeps cars from just running across the Highway in Shuba.

"What are you gonna' do?"

"I don't know," I said softly. "Maybe I can ask the minister—"

Don's voice was ragged. "I keep thinkin' of how you looked with no clothes on. You want to come with me— away from here, to the county seat, maybe?"

I took a deep breath. He had on a suit and a white shirt, and he smelled nice. I remembered I was still hanging to his little pistol. I reached to put it in his hand. My thigh rubbed lightly against him. I felt his muscles tighten. "Might as well tell you," I said. "I never been with a man before—any man. I wouldn't rightly know how to do it. I thank you for helping me when I needed it, Don Carson, but I don't suppose I better go with you."

He patted his face with his handkerchief, turned towards me on the seat. His knees touched mine. "Listen," he said, "Listen. I—I can't stop seeing you all naked and white aganst the wall. I can't stop seeing you like a tiny devil, shootin' your folks to save me from getting my head knocked in. Lee—you swear what you say is true? You swear that you never had a man before them?"

I nodded, and his hand closed gently over mine. His fingers were trembling.

"How-how old are you?" he asked.

I told him I was fifteen.

He squeezed my hand. "Listen—I know a Justice of the Peace over to Quitmill. We don't need a license with him. In just a few minutes, we can be outa' his place and on our way to a fine motel. I'll-I'll be good to you, Lee. I swear I will."

"What—what are you—"

"I'm askin' you to marry me. I'm being honest and doing things right. I'm all shook up over you, Lee Green. I—I just can't stand the idea of you goin' off alone."

"M—marry me?" I couldn't believe it. This only happened in books. But Don was clinging to my hand, pushing his knees against mine and breathing hard.

Maybe this was as it should be, I thought. He'd come out of the night as a stranger, to save me from what Pete and Jett were fixing to do. He'd stood up to a shotgun with his little pistol. Now Don Carson was asking me to marry him. I could get away from Shuba. I could have nice clothes and another pair of shoes. I could go where the town people wouldn't point me out and poke fun at me.

"All right," I said, "If you're certain sure you want me."

He was shaking all over when he leaned to kiss me. His mouth was warm and soft. I liked the way he kissed me. I liked the tender touch of his hands on my breasts. Don didn't maul my breasts, just stroked them. I kissed him back, squirming, eager, pushing to him. He finally pulled back and started up the car.

"We better hurry," he said.

A hell of a weekend for a young, mixed-up kid, wasn't it? Ma's death, getting raped, and a stranger for a husband. Oh yes—and something else had happened that was going to have a profound influence upon the rest of my life.

I had shot my first two men, and found it was as easy as plinking a pair of fat rabbits.

Easier.

CHAPTER FOUR

Huddling between soft, almost-new sheets, cuddled in the springiest bed I had ever known, I waited for my new husband to come to me. The room was beautiful; excitement swept over me in waves, not unmixed with a spicy sence of adventure, and a Vague, edge-of-consciousness gnawing of guilt. After all, I had only known the man in the bathroom for less then two hours. Fretfully, I thought there should be more to marriage than this, more than standing before a sleepy-cyed man in a torn undershirt while he mumbled a few words from memory an said, I-now-pronounce-you-man-and-wife-five-dollars-please.

I got all shaky inside, and breathing hard, and sort of hunching on his hand because I liked it, and then he turned us over so that I was lying on top of him.

"Like this, baby," he said. "This way, baby. Take in in your hand—that's it, oh, that's it. Push it into your little pussy, baby. Yeah, oh yeah—like that and like this and ain't that the sweetest, tightest, hottest little pussy anybody ever saw; Do it, little girl—do it good!"

I did it the best I knew how, working his thing up inside my tender vagina and moving up and down on him while he lay there with his eyes closed and his head thrown back and his legs spread wide. It got to be good for me, slicky and wiggly and that enjoyable dirty feeling. I bounced harder and faster on his thing, and kind of ground it around and around so that he'd get the feel of every part of my vagina, and so that he'd rub against my clitoris better. Of course, back then I didn't even know the names of those parts of me, but I knew what felt good, and I sure humped and squirmed, riding him like he was a stud horse.

"Baby!" he hollered out loud, and grabbed my buttocks as he came. I took a few more strokes and made it with him, throbbing all over my body, quivering and gasping at how wonderful it all was, at how sweet and lovely it could be.

Gently, my new husband rolled me off him and spread me tenderly upon the bed like I was a Sunday dinner getting ready for him. Because that's just how he went at me next, like a hungry man who couldn't ever get enough meat to eat. Not that he gobbled, because he didn't. He took his time and went all over me, savoring the flavor and texture of my flesh.

Don kissed my throat and shoulders; he kissed and sucked upon my breasts, and not just the nipples. He tried to take the entire mound into his mouth, and the hot, wet feeling of that made me wriggle and bounce upon the mattress. He slid on down my body to my belly, licking with his tongue, nipping easy like with his teeth. When he put his tongue into my navel, I almost went out of my head. I held to his hair and rolled my hips, and wished I knew better what he truly wanted me to do.

Then he was down there between my legs, kissing and biting lightly on the tender skin inside my thighs. I shook and trembled, waiting for something I knew vaguely was coming, wanting it, needing it. Don brought me along just so far, then his mouth found my cleft and I was transported into a new and devastating kind of ecstacy. Thrill after thrill shot through me, and it was only moments later that I reached a tremendous orgasm that left me half-fainting and limp upon my wedding bed.

It was so wonderful. Don had been so kind to me, so thrilling. He made me feel like a princess, like someone he worshipped. Nobody had ever treated me that way before, and I thought he was just about perfect. So I didn't mind at all when he wanted me to take his thing into my mouth; it was just a turnaround. I could make him as happy as he had just made me, and he was my own true husband, so it was different from the ugliness that Pete had tried to make me do.

I went down on Don. I tried everything I could think of to make him happy with me, to give him ecstacy. I used my hands and fingers, my tongue and my teeth and a suction that seemed to excite him more than anything else. I was completely his and he was mine all the way, and we were husband and wife. We were all legal and all respectable, and if he had wanted me to run up the walls backwards and naked as a jaybird, I'd sure as hell have tried it for him.

So when he released himself into my mouth, I accepted that as part of being married and waited awhile to turn my head from him. Funny; I never did enjoy doing that for a man. I've done it a lot of times since, of course, but it just doesn't thrill me as some women claim it does to them. Maybe I'm built differently, but I go down on a man because I love him—or I think I do, or because I'm trying to lull any suspicious he might have about who and what and why I am.

I don't do it for kicks, and sometimes I hate the idea almost as bad as that first time when Pete had it in his hand and was trying to force it between my tightly clamped lips. But love or hate, I do it sometimes, and the man concerned sure as hell can't tell the difference.

But I'm wandering again. Back to my new husband and the sensual fling we had that first night of marriage. I petted Don and loved him, and tried to be all things to him until we both just sort of wore out.

Later, I didn't mind when Don switched on the bed lamp and checked the sheets. I guessed it was his right to see if I had been telling him the truth. I hadn't acted like a just-about virgin, tearing at him like that, meeting his every move with passionate hunger and a need that more than matched his own. But I hadn't lied to Don, and he saw for himself. I was still tender enought to bleed.

He smiled at me and reached for his shorts. "There's some salve in the bathroom," he said. "I got it when I stopped at the drugstore. You can use it after you take a shower. You know how to work a shower?"

"I reckon," I said. "It can't be too hard."

Then I blushed, but Don wasn't looking. He was working the cork out of a bottle of liquor. I took my dress off the chair.

"Never mind that," he said. "I like to watch you walk. And I'll be waitin' for you."

Luxuriating under the warm, cleansing spray of the glass-and-tile shower, I felt more alive than I'd ever been. I felt gay and wonderful. At last, I was my own woman. No more dodging the sly hands of Pete and Jett Finney; no more slinking shamefaced to school because I didn't have shoes. I was Mrs. Don Carson, and I rolled the beautiful name around in my mouth tasting it, reveling in its flavor.

Now I didn't ever have to creep into Shuba stores again, reddening under the smirking grins of the potbellied men behind the counters piled so high with things I could never have. I didn't have to stalk a winter-thinned possum so I could eat. I didn't have to do anything but be a good and loving wife to my man.

That sounds simple, doesn't it? Well, nothing is ever so uncomplicated in life with a smalltime conman like Don Carson. United Farm Machinery salesman, country drummer, joke-cracking, shine-drinking grifter who always had an eye out for one thing—an angle to help Don Carson climb just a bit higher the "easy" way.

Maybe he loved me as much as he was capable of loving any-one. I don't know. But I do know that his kind of "love" wasn't strong enough to stand up under the temptation of a fifty dollar raise. Fifty lousy dollars a month was the price for Don selling out his own wife.

And I mean that literally. I'll go into detail about it, because I want to remember it all myself, go every cunning, degrading event that I was pushed into by my husband. But first, I have to backtrack, to explain how it was in the beginning.

Don was on the road most of the time, and he didn't want to be tied down to a real house. He got special rates from the motel, and I tried to make the one room and bath as much like a home as I could. I didn't complain, because it was a hell of a lot better than the shack in the woods. But I missed him, when he was gone for two and three nights at a time. I got magazines from the motel owner and read them eagerly from cover. I read newspa-pers and a book about Alaska some traveler had left behind. And I waited for Don to come back.

When he did, I'd hurry to him and kiss him hard, the way he liked. And I'd always be fresh and clean, and wearing one of the pretty cotton dresses he'd bought me. For the first few weeks, we'd go right to bed, even if it was broad daylight, and we'd make love until we were all loved out.

Don would talk to me, after—telling me about his job and how hard it was to get to be a district manager. I'd listen, munching on a hamburger and potato chips from the diner across the road. Finally, I asked him if there was anything I could do to help.

He looked at me for a long time. "No," he said. "Not yet. You still make too many mistakes, still act like a piney woods girl."

I started to tell him I was practicing every day, but he cut me off.

"Yeah, I know. And I'll take you to a company party soon as I think you're ready. Then you can help me, baby. Then you can really help your husband get up in the world. If you want to."

"Oh, I want to," I said. "I really want to. Any way I can. I'd do anything for you, Don."

"Remember that," he said. "You may have to."

I didn't know what he meant then. But the first company party he ever took me to wasn't halfway over before I had an idea. We'd no more than got inside the door of this big house in the city of Merid, than Don pulled me into a corner.

"Push the front of your dress a little lower," he whispered.

"Huh? Don, I—"

"Shut up. These ain't redneck farmers here. They like to see some woman flesh. Now you do like I told you, and you listen close. You see that fat man by the bar? Well, you play up to him. Be real nice to Mister Holcomb. If he—likes you, it might mean my promotion."

I stared up at Don. "You mean, flirt with him?"

His hand tightened on my elbow. "Yeah, yeah. Mister Holcomb's got an eye for pretty young wives. Dance with him, and he'll get you out on the porch. Don't worry, I'll make myself scarce. If he wants to kiss you, go ahead. Play up to him. Do whatever you have to, you hear?"

I swallowed. "You—you don't mean—"

But Don wasn't listening. He was shoving me at the fat man, gabbling an introduction, pushing a glass into my hand. I put the glass to my lips and drank all of the sweet red stuff it held, needing time to think, to adjust. Surely, Don couldn't mean he wanted his wife to—to—"You're a mighty pretty girl," Mister Holcomb purred. "Have another Singapore Sling. They're real weak."

There was a warmth already spreading in my stomach. I wasn't used to drinking. Just the stink of mash cooking back in the woods used to make me queasy. But Mister Holcomb was right. The Sling tasted like cherry pop. It couldn't hurt me. I drank the next one down, and looked around for Don. He was gone.

"You do all right for such a little girl," Mister Holcomb said. "Have another, and we'll dance some."

"Sure," I giggled. After all, I was only doing as Don said. I was playing up to the man who could make my husband a manager.

On the floor, Mister Holcomb kept putting his knee in between my legs, and rubbing his swollen belly into me. Every time I tried to pull back, he held me closer. His breath was tickling my neck. I missed a step and said "whoo!"

"My, my," he said and led me to the open porch. "I guess it's too hot in there. Maybe we better walk around back while you cool off some."

That sounded like a good idea. My head was spinning and my feet wouldn't work right. I thought those Sling drinks were a mite stronger than I'd figured. Before I knew it, I was sitting on the grass behind some thick azalea bushes and Mister Holcomb had his hand on my leg.

"M—my dress," I said thickly. "I'll get my dress all stained."

He rubbed my thigh. "I'll buy you another dress. You're the prettiest little thing I've ever seen. Yes sir, I guess old Don is a lucky man."

My head bobbed on a loose neck; my eyes were blurred, and I could barely feel Mister Holcomb's face nuzzling at my breasts.

"Don't," I said. "Please don't. Don—my husband—"

Mister Holcomb stopped playing. "Don't kid me," he said. "Old Don ain't coming back right away. He wants that manager's job too bad. You want it too, Mrs. Carson?"

"I—I don't know what you mean—"

"Sure you do. Didn't old Don tell you to be nice to me? Well, you better be nice as you know how, and I mean right away. Or else your husband can forget about the job."

The azalea bushes swam in a hazy fog. Mr. Holcomb worked his fingers down. The elastic band snapped. His mouth was hard on mine, prying my lips apart. I didn't know, I didn't know.

There was grass under my naked hips, damp in the evening dew. My skirt was up to my chin. There was no tenderness, no sweet caressing—only the dark, greedy hammering of his body, only the sickening alien soiling and whinnying that made me twist my face into the cooling grass.

"Thatsa' way, baby. Over on your belly; I like to feel a broad's ass up to me when I ram her. Lift it, baby—lift it, damn you. There—that's better. Take ol' Holcomb's rod into you like that—ah, yes. Hot little bitch, ain't you?"

He pumped away after he got me propped on my hands and knees, after he got me set to his satisfaction. Mister Holcomb thought he was a real bull, and the liquor he'd had made him rougher, but he truly wasn't much; he was just greedy and selfish and hammered into me like I was a breeding heifer in heat.

Don had never done it to me that particular fashion, so I made it better by pretending I enjoyed it, and before long, that was the truth. I waggled my butt and shook it for him, and Mister Holcomb hunched and panted on me the best he could. I felt him up inside me, and clamped on him the way I'd learned Don liked.

He kind of moaned and let go—just that quick. He left me without an orgasm of my own, and I hated him for that, for taking me as if I was so much blank-minded meat, without regard to my own feelings, my own needs. Then the bastard had ideas about oral gratification—his, of course. But when he crawled around and tried to make me take it into my mouth, I turned my head away and spat.

"Suck it," he said.

"No," I said. "You've done enough to me, mister."

He stared at me in the dark. I could feel his mean little eyes trying to read my face, trying to find out if I meant what I said, and maybe an edge had sneaked into my voice. He decided I was serious, that there'd be no more free goodies for him, oral or otherwise.

"Okay," Mister Holcomb hissed. "Pull down your damned dress. Before you come back to the party, brush yourself off, clean up some. And you can tell your husband I ain't so sure about the manager's opening. You weren't too nice to me."

He left me sobbing dry-eyed in the dark. The bittersweet taste of the drinks boiled in my throat, and I sat up to retch into the bushes. I don't remember how long I choked and gasped there, before staggering off toward our car parked behind the house. I sat there waiting for Don, but he didn't come. I couldn't drive the car, so I got out and walked all the way back to the motel.

In the shower, I scrubbed and scrubbed, but the feel of dirt wouldn't come off. I crawled into bed, telling myself that Don hadn't meant for me to do that, that he only wanted me to flirt with his boss and lead him on. It was my fault for drinking so much, for going out in the dark with Mister Holcomb. Don didn't have to know. I wouldn't hurt him by telling him how no good I had been. I'd just tell him I got sick and came home.

I didn't have to tell my husband anything. He came storming through the door a few minutes later, staggering drunk. He wasn't alone. Mister Holcomb was right behind him. I froze as Don leaned over and jerked the sheet from my naked body.

"Wench," he muttered, "Tryin' louse me up, actin' like you don't know how. Tol' Mister Holcomb you're hot stuff, and you're gonna' prove it. I'm gonna' see you prove it, you hear?"

It was Pete and Jett Finney all over again—and old one and a young one, holding me, pawing at me not wanting me as an individual, as a woman to be loved. They only wanted me as a thing to be used for their own perverted gratification. My husband, my lover, the knight who had rescued me from the pain and horror. Now he was bringing the horror to me, forcing it upon me.

I didn't fight. There wasn't anything to fight for. Whatever there had been was lost in the drunken looseness of Don's face, in the fumbling hands that were readying my body for another man. All right, I thought wildly. All right, damn you!

And I didn't just accept Mister-Holcomb. I took him: I did every damned thing to him that I had ever done for Don. It wasn't love, and it wasn't passion, but a deep, driving hate that made me grind my hips wantonly, that forced me to claw and moan and rock the bed with my gyrating body. Mister Holcomb wasn't conquering me. I was conquering him, taking him, proving my hate and my superiority over his weakly rutting body. He was a symbol of all men, of all erotic dirt that needed to be beaten and ground under my heels. And I beat him. I made him stagger protesting from the bed with his obscenely nude belly quivering.

I looked triumphantly at my husband, my pimp, my true love. He was snoring in a chair. His shirt was stained with sweat and—I looked closer—with lipstick, too. Good old Don Carson had been busy, himself. Was there another wife feeling sick somewhere just now; Or just another wench who'd had herself a hell of a good time?

Mister Holcomb was lifting weary legs into his shorts. I stood there with my hands on my naked, sweaty hips and laughed at him.

"Ah—Lee—" he said.

"You tired old man," I said. "Did you have enough? Hell—a little bit would be more than enough for you. I don't want you to forget about the manager's job, Mister Holcomb. Because if Don doesn't come home on Monday and tell me he's got it, I'm going down to the company and let everybody know just how good you're not. You understand me, Mister Holcomb?"

"You—you wouldn't dare—"

"Try me," I said. "My self respect crawled under the bed the moment my husband brought you in here. Just try me."

He was tugging at his pants as he went out the door. "A-all right, Lee. All right."

I stared at the door after he'd gone. I looked down at Don's dangling hand and saw a half-filled bottle of liquor on the floor beside it. I took the bottle and drank from it. The stuff didn't make me feel sick. I balanced the bottle in my hand and picked a spot on Don's head. Then I decided that just hating a man wasn't enough. I had to be practical. If Don Carson could move up in business, if he could make more money by trading his wife's body, then I could do it, too. Why the hell should I be left with the short end of the stick? I wanted to get away from Don Carson, away from the state of Mississippi.

And now I realized just how I could do it.

CHAPTER FIVE

If you're wondering just what the hell all this background has to do with Lee Carson today, you haven't ever opened a sociology textbook. Environment, it's called, plus learned traits stemming from trauma.

See? I read more than comic books, in the years since I ran away from that farm with Don Carson. The professors might have an answer for that, too—something about a compulsion to dominate. All I knew was that if I wanted to stay a step ahead of men, I had to be smarter than they were. I got smarter by reading and absorbing everything I could lay my hands on.

I had some help along the way. First from my cheap grifter husband, who wanted me "acceptable" for the company parties—acceptable meaning being able to wear shoes and refraining from eating with my fingers. The real help came from a guy who had plenty to give.

Roy Warner was a graduate of Ole Miss, and vice president of United Farm Machinery through stock inheritance. But he'd probably have made it on his own—if he'd known how to stop being a nice, gentle guy. Nice, yes, and still a man, with all the unconscious arrogance of the male who isn't really sure of himself deep down. On Roy, the arrogance didn't show, but it was there all the same. As most any man, he had the idea that he could buy and sell women as he might deal in livestock.

I suppose he was right, in general. Where I was concerned, anyhow. But I got the better end of the bargain, by far. Roy's profit was only sex tailored to his particular specifications; my profit was more lasting. Trading with Roy Warner brought me everything that truly counts—money, poise and knowledge. I might say that Roy was the gatekeeper to the door that opened on the big and glamorous world, and he showed me how to pass through. For weeks after the messy incidents in the azalea bushes and the motel room, I had been forced to act the meek and submissive wife to Don Carson, to tacitly pretend that nothing out of the ordinary had happened with Mister Holcomb. What the hell else could I do? I had no money, only a few bargain sale dresses, no place to go. Sure, I could have begged a job serving beer and hamburgers in some sleazy juke joint for five bucks a week and tips. Don't you think I'd have had to warm a few beds to keep working?

Roy Warner was a much easier way out, and a much better way. I met him at another party, a gathering where the company big brass awed and subdued the rank and file with their illustrious presence. Later I found that the big boys usually stayed at their own ornate table, untouchable within their own magic circle. I didn't realize that Roy Warner was breaking precedent by asking me to dance. Once on the floor, I did realize there was more polish to this man, a touch of quiet refinement that made the others seem like inept fumblers.

Roy was a short, slim man, only a few inches above my own five-two. He was dark, with straight black hair and direct eyes. I thought he'd chosen me because he didn't like the other big women towering over him, and that could have partly been the reason. But we seemed to fit, right from the start. I felt every movement of his body, instinctively knowing each change of rhythm. I pillowed my face lightly against his chest. He smelled of expensive shaving lotion and imported material. I felt his breath stir the hair over my ear.

"You're the loveliest woman in the room," he said.

I didn't lift my face. "Thank you."

Roy spun me slowly about the floor. "I believe in being direct. I want you, Mrs. Lee Carson—not for a quick and sweaty few minutes, not for a too-short and stolen night in a shabby motel room. I want you all to myself, with plenty of time to know each other, with plenty of time to adapt ourselves."

He was direct, all right. I liked it. "I won't pretend I'm shocked, mister. I may be young, but I've grown up a lot in the past few months. What's your offer?"

There was no break in the smooth gliding of our feet on the dance floor. "Leave your husband and move in with me. I can arrange a long road trip through several states for our new manager, so he won't be around to bother us. You're much too beautiful for such a clod."

"And for the other clod, too? For Mister Holcomb?"

"I wasn't going to mention that," Roy said.

"But you knew. I won't make excuses for that. It happened, but not again. So I move in with you while my husband's gone. What then? When he comes back, do I say thank you for a nice time and forget it?"

Roy chuckled. "I give you more credit. Lee, you're the kind of woman men lose their heads over. You have a certain, intangible aura about you, a spicy attraction that makes men want to touch you. But unless you improve yourself, you'll just remain as you are, and no more. You'll stay a sexy little bountry girl until you're grey and fat and the magic is all gone. But there are bigger, more exciting things in store for you—if you want them badly enough."

The music stopped. I walked with Roy out to the veranda, ignoring venomous stares of other women. "Such as?" I asked.

He didn't touch me, didn't try to kiss me. Roy was shrewd. He knew that the most sexually sensitive part of a woman is her

mind. He just talked to me, intriguing me by his surface coolness, making me want to force him into physical proof of his
desire for me.

"Such as travel," he said, "Such as the opportunity to meet
rich and lonely men. If you're good as you look, Lee, I can promise
you training that will help you move through the better classes.
When you're ready I have friends on the West Coast who run a
model agency. I'll see that you get a job there, plus living expenses
while you're getting started. Does that sound interesting?"

"It sounds wonderful," I said. "I'm direct, too—let's go home,
Roy."

He blinked. "Right now?"

"Right now. Don will be sure to look the other way. After all,
you're the vice-president."

Roy laughed. "You're improving already. As you say, Mrs.
Carson—let's go home."

I didn't even send for my toothbrush. I did call from Roy's
bachelor cottage and leave a message at the motel for my husband: "Hope you enjoy your trip." That was all. The hell with Don
Carson, with the ratty room I'd called home, with two ninety-
eight cotton dresses and playing up to lecherous old men. Lee
Carson was on her way—somewhere. Anywhere I went would
be a step up.

When I put down the telephone, I turned and smiled at Roy.
"Okay, where do we start?"

He said huskily, low in his throat: "Here and now, with the
lights bright and the curtains drawn. Take off your clothes, Lee;
take them off slowly and gracefully, piece by piece. I want to see
that lovely body stripped by degrees, so that I can enjoy each
step."

I shrugged. Why not? Roy was paying the freight, or would
be. He could have me just the way he wanted, with whatever frills

he liked. I didn't feel ashamed or shy. There had been a basic change in me, ever since the affair with Holcomb, ever since I had to return to my husband's arms as if I was still his ever-loving bride. Now my body was a tool, a weapon for my advantage. Love with synonymous with lie. Love was only a four-letter word. So was hate. Only hate was stronger.

I pealed out of my sheer blouse, stood posed for a long moment before unzipping my thin skirt and letting it fall to the floor. My slip was cheap and stiff, but I filled it out well. Pirouetting slowly, I lifted the hem over my head and swirled the slip away. Arms out, back arched, legs spread wide, I stood before Roy in a bra and panties.

His dark face was intense, a tight smile fixed on his smooth lips. There was a tall glass in his hand. I heard the ice rattle. Reaching up and behind, I unsnapped the bra hook. Roy caught his breath. I took three, long, gliding steps toward his chair. Then I dropped the last bit of clothing and lifted one foot at a time out of them.

Roy's hands closed, on the flare of my hips. He pulled me gently down to him. My mouth fastened to his; my fingers were swift and deft at buttons. I remembered something he had said, words about if I was as good as I looked. Roy had been around. He was no corny salesman, no fat desk man. I had to prove myself to him, make myself everything he could possibly want.

We moved from the chair to the floor, to coil together on a spotless white rug. In the beginning, I took my time, sensing his needs, blending myself into his desires. Roy was agile, experienced, in no hurry. I moved this way for him, moved that way, building a whitehot heat within myself that I could soon no longer deny. Its explosion was overwhelming, sweeping us both before it.

My imagination ran riot. It no longer mattered what Roy wanted, but what I wanted. I became the aggressor, thrusting, taking, fighting to slash and bite and crush. I clenched him with all the angry strength in my legs, held him to me with all the hating power of my arms. When the powerful, shattering heights were reached, I had this weaker man-thing pinned beneath me, my teeth locked savagely into his shoulder, shaking him with brutal force, triumphant.

When the thunder had died away, when the hurricane winds had gone, I was afraid. I thought everything would be over, that surely this man had felt my scorn, the bitterness of my attack. I thought Roy Warner would tell me to get out.

Of course, he didn't. He sighed away from me, sated and momentarily drained. I didn't know then that the vast majority of men want to be fought against, they need to be despised and hated and mastered. Naturally they don't realize this. They lie to themselves, rationalize away any gnawings of misgiving. They pretend they have been the strong, the unquenchable, the conquerors. They conjure up the image that their strength and adoitness were the reasons that women turned so wanton and wild.

So much for my "mistake" with Roy Warner. Instead of turning him against me, it inflated his sick ego, made him proud that his rare touch could turn a shy girl into a raging inferno of raw, lustful sex. We didn't put on any clothes, but lounged around his luxurious cottage in the nude, drinking imported champagne and dancing to exotic music. Later that night, we stood together under the shower, playing tickly games and soap and water and flesh. And we slept at last in a massive bed made with satin sheets the color of fire.

I didn't hear from my husband for almost three weeks, and it surprised me. I had almost forgotten I had a husband. Roy and I were meshing so beautifully, blending so well with each other. And I had been busy with other interesting things—study, acquiring a taste in clothes, reading books on etiquette, practicing how to walk, trying new hair-dos, different methods of making up my face. Roy's advice was invaluable; he always knew the right way. It was easy for him; he had been born to the knowing.

Don's message said he was coming home for a short stay. He wanted me to meet him. I showed the telegram to Roy.

"What do you want to do?" he asked.

I shrugged. "Ignore him, I guess. Can't you ship him back out, right away?"

Roy smiled. "Certainly. I'll wire back and change his orders as of now, if that's what you want."

"I want," I said. "I don't give a damn if I never see Don Carson again."

I didn't know it then, but I'd see plenty of my husband in the future. I would see so damned much of him that his continued, nagging presence would push me into saying something I didn't fully mean.

And that one irritated statement I was going to make would commit me irrevocably to the underworld. It would also cost Don Carson his life.

CHAPTER SIX

I didn't let go of the seat arms until the plane had been in the air for a long time. It was my first time off the ground, and the flight scared hell out of me. I still don't like flying, but often it's a must.

Leaning back in the tilted seat, I tried to relax. I guess the tension showed, but when the man in the seat beside me said something meant to be kind, I kept my eyes closed and pretended not to hear him.

I thought about Roy Warner, about how he'd looked at the airport, how he'd sounded. When I left Roy back in Merid, he was a different man from the one who'd so cooly propositioned me on a dance floor. But then, I was a different woman, too.

With his help, I'd learned fast, and the lessons weren't all concerning what to say and how to dress and what to do among the rich. Some of the knowledge was passed on without Roy knowing it. We had been together for almost a year. He'd kept my husband traveling, bribing him with occasional raises and fancier titles. Don Carson didn't give a damn about the naive kid he'd left behind, and that worked both ways. The kid who'd turned into a shrewd and somewhat polished woman didn't give a damn about him, either. The longer he stayed away, the better I liked it.

When I decided I was ready to move on, I forced Roy Warner into backing up his promises. He was reluctant to let me go, and that was understandable. Few men can find a woman who is wife, mistress and symbolic mother to them. But Roy kept holding to his casual facade right up until the last minute. I understood this part of him, too. He was the man of the world, educated, intelligent, monied. I was only something he had created, a personality he'd put together over the months. I wasn't real. At least, not real enough to be accepted by his friends and upper class business associates.

Roy was the last of an old-line family; his blood was as blue as any of that in Kentucky or Virginia. They had plantations and wooded empires in his background. The Warner name was prominently inscribed on scrolls of honor that covered five wars. It was unthinkable that it be linked with any other than one just as old and respected.

But he asked me to marry him. Standing there just outside the terminal, Roy Warner asked me to marry him, blurting it out against his will, mixing the proposal with talk of a trip around the world, of lazing away the coming years in far places of the sun. If he hadn't said the rest, I might have agreed. I knew what the travel talk was, what it really meant. It meant he'd legalize our relationship but not in Mississippi. It meant I was still the daughter of a redneck dirt farmer, that I'd be a nameless divorcee shunned by his friends if we stayed in the bigoted, narrow Cradle of the Confederacy.

His thick book of Travelers' Checks was in my purse, along with a letter of introduction to the Dowers Model Agency, along with a sheaf of bills for pin money and tipping. Already on the plane, my luggage was costly and packed tight with fashionable dresses. I stood in a mist of fifty dollar an ounce perfume.

I said, "No, Roy—I won't marry you. I still have a husband, remember?"

"Don't joke, Lee. I'm serious. I'll pay off Don, make him divorce you. We can be married in Reno."

My smile was thin, reserved. On the strip, the big jet taxied into position. It looked clean and bright. "Why not be married in Merid?" I asked. "We can make it a big thing, the social event of the season."

Roy flushed. "Now, Lee—"

I stuck out my hand. "Thanks. Thanks a lot. It's been fun."

"Lee—please—"

High heels tapping briskly, I strode through the ticket gate and up the ramp with a casualness I didn't feel. It was like crossing a bridge that was going to be swept away behind me. There could be no turning back. I didn't wave at Roy. My final salute was mental and silent, a kiss-off to red clay and a flat belly, to smelly sharecroppers and moonshine-brave rapists, to a husband who used his one-girl stable to move up in the world. Squeezing my eyes shut, I clung to the seat arms as the plane trembled forward with a thunderous hiss and swept up from the earth.

"I said—you can smoke now," the voice said at my ear. "It helps."

A rough voice, untained with the slurred nasality of the South; a voice with a cold sense of unlimited power in its husky tones. I looked into the face that went with it. That was cold, too.

"Thanks, guess I was a little frightened. It's my first trip."

I took his cigarette and held it into the flame of his gold lighter. The fingers holding it were uncalloused, the nails clipped short and polished. Crisp black hairs curled on the back of his hand.

"Good," I said. "There's some truth in the TV commercials after all. I do feel more relaxed."

He nodded. "I'm Mel Tani. I already know your name. The stewardess showed me the flight manifest. Was that your husband back there, Mrs. Carson?"

Jolted, I said, "N—no. He's—I mean, my husband and I are—separated."

"My turn to say good. I like to know just how things stand."

"Look, Mr. Tani—"

"Mel."

"All right, Mel. I'm not certain I like your sudden interest in my affairs."

He smiled. The white flash of even teeth broke the harsh planes of his blocky face, changed it from a study in hard watchfulness. Now it was a nice face, open and compelling. I had to smile back at him.

"Okay," I said. "I'll admit I'm interested by your interest, and I'm glad to have someone to talk to. I'm still afraid to look out the window."

We talked for a long time, just chatting, feeling each other out, not prying. It was good to be able to relax with a man, to be friends with him, even if that friendship was prevented from progressing into anything else by the fact that we were twenty-thousand feet in the air, surrounded by other passengers.

Mel gave me a business card. The embossed lettering read: "The Club Tani." I told him I had him placed as an executive, not a nightclub owner. That pleased him, because the rare smile lighted his face again.

"It's not a bad business," he said. "I do all right with the club. You know, Lee—if that modeling job you mentioned happens to go sour, I'd be honored if you'd call on me. I can always use beautiful girls in the club. Nothing you wouldn't like, of course. You could be window dressing. The suckers—the customers, that is—like to watch a lovely woman. They buy more, just day-dreaming."

I laughed. "I don't sing very well, and my dancing is strictly limited. I'm afraid I'll have to pass up your offer, Mel—although

I'm happy you made it, really. But I have a letter to the Dowers Agency, and I'm not broke. I'm sure everything will work out."

He nodded at the card. "Put that in your purse, anyway. You never can tell."

I continued to sense something alien about Mel Tani, a hing my woman's intuition couldn't quite pin down. Accustomed to Roy Warner's precisely chosen words, I could distinguish a strange combination of dialects in Mel's—a careful diction that sometimes slipped and let in stray terms of toughness. But I supposed that was because of his work, his club. He'd meet many kinds of people there, and they wouldn't all be good ones.

There was another thing. Any time another passenger moved down the aisle to the rest rooms, Mel watched, turning back to me only when the person was out of sight. He seemed vaguely on edge, somehow cautious. I pushed the idea away. After all, what did I know about people like Mel Tani? My world had been limited until now. But I was branching out. I was going to become part of a new existance.

It was early in the morning when we reached Los Angeles. The city was a glistening wonderland below us as we came smoothly in for a landing. I was entranced, excited as a schoolgirl. This city would open its arms to me. It would be mine to taste. It wasn't too big a step from being a model to being a movie star. Hollywood, Beverly Hills, lowslung sports cars and pink champagne. I barely heard Mel Tani's regretful goodbye.

I stared out of the taxi window, trying to absorb it all at once. In the hotel, I was too jumpy to nap. I bathed and ordered breakfast in my room, and picked out my very best daytime dress. When the Dowers Model Agency opened its doors that morning, I was first at the receptionist's desk. One look at the sleek, poised, and fullbodied girl, and my heart sank. If a girl who looked like that was working at a desk—

My letter from Roy got me into the inner offices. I felt tiny, and insignificant after following the hipshifting tallness of the receptionist into Mr. Dower's sanctum. But I stood as tall as I could, telling myself that size didn't really matter in pictures.

Mr. Dowers was sleek, too, hair shiny as a cat's and every strand in place. "Have a seat, darling," he said. "I've been expecting you."

The "darling" put me off balance, until I remembered that everybody around Hollywood is supposed to talk like that. It doesn't mean anything.

I posed on the edge of a deep leather chair, my skirt just a bit over my knees. "Expecting me?"

He propped one hip on the edge of a white desk. "Roy called me yesterday. He thinks a lot of you, darling."

"I know, but—"

"But you have this driving desire to conquer Hollywood, right? Lee, darling, this town is crawling with beautiful girls, and I mean literally. I suppose you saw Gloria outside?"

I nodded. "She's very—"

"Tall and sexy and she photographs well. Not quite well enough to be a top model, of course. Just enough to pose for girlie shots for the men's magazines. Not much money in that."

"Mr. Dowers," I said slowly, "Mr. Dowers, darling; are you trying to tell me something? Such as Roy Warner putting thumbs-down on a job for me here?"

He touched one eyebrow with a shaped fingernail, "You'll be much better off, you know. Roy has scads of money, and he seems to be in love with you."

I stood up, feeling the warmth in my face, the weakness in my legs and the familiar hatred bubbling inside me. Men—even semi-men such as this one—men pushing buttons and pulling strings and expecting me to bow and scrape. The hell I would.

"All right, dear," I said through stiff lips. "You know what you can do with your job, don't you?"

Then I told him, in short ugly words that made him gasp and flutter his white hands. I banged the door behind me when I went out. My spirits sank with the elevator as it took me back down to the ground floor. Roy Warner hadn't been able to take no for an answer. He thought if he pinched off the easy chance for me, that I'd come running back. No. I wouldn't go back. In Mississippi I was white trash. In Los Angeles I was as good as anyone else.

I rode a cab back to the hotel and though of what I was going to do. Dowers had been right about one thing—Hollywood was overrun with lovely girls. I saw them behind lunch counters and running elevators and car-hopping at drive-ins. The odds were too big to buck, without help.

So what was left? Reaching into my purse for cigarettes, I found Mel Tani's card.

That night, my first in California, I walked into the Club Tani, and straight into a shadowy subworld where violence and death are as common as breathing. There, life is a commodity, bought, sold and discarded without emotion. There, the professional gunner, the "hitter," is prince to the all-powerful kings of crime who use their services to put down rebellions and punish troublesome subjects.

Mel Tani was one of the black princes, a hired killer.

CHAPTER SEVEN

It's not tough to be a stripper. Only the theatrical union doesn't like that word; they prefer "exotic dancer." Anyway, all it takes is the right distribution of flesh, a streak of exhibitionism and a certain sense of rhythm. Enough to move smoothly and keep time with the drums.

Damned near any girl can look good under a blue spotlight, and they seem downright appealing through the bleared eyes of drunks at ringside tables. I didn't have any trouble, after getting together such costumes as were called for, learning to apply makeup thickly, and throwing myself into those first lusty bumps and grinds.

Mel didn't want me to work, but I think he respected me for insisting. To Mel, I had that certain indefinable something he called "class." Maybe it was the liquid accent I was trying to shake, or the right thing approach imparted to me by Roy Warner's centuries of breeding. Whatever it was, Mel was fascinated by me. And he could have had his pick of a hundred willing girls, bigger, chestier, longer-limbed. He wanted Lee Carson, and that was all right with me.

When I walked into the Club Tani that first evening, Mel almost skipped toward me. Holding my hand between his, he said, "I'm glad, Lee. Maybe it's wrong to say so, but I'm glad the model job didn't work out."

"It would have," I said. "If a certain guy hadn't called it off."

"The airport guy?"

I nodded. "You said you could use a girl here—for window dressing?"

"Sure, sure, but—" he released my hand. "—But you don't have to work, Lee. Not if you don't want to."

I looked at him, at the dark and heavy-lidded eyes. "I won't play coy and pretend I don't know what you're talking about, Mel. Apartment, charge account, the works. With you, it would be that way—all out. But I can't just sit on my hands. I'd like to keep busy; and I'd like to earn my own money. Okay?"

White and wide, the rare smile opened up his face. "Sure; anything you say, Lee—anything. You—you mean the rest of it's all right? The apartment, me?"

Slowly, I nodded. "I'm grateful, Mel, and flattered. I think you and I will make a good pair."

"You bet," he said. "You can make book on that."

So it was that simple, a proposition made and accepted. Mel and I left the club early that night, and I stood by while he keyed the door to his apartment. It was plush, and just a bit overdone by my newly-learned standards of taste. The place was also obviously expensive.

Mel Tani was big and tough, but standing in his own living room and facing me, he shifted from foot to foot like a small boy. "Lee—if you don't feel up to–I mean, well, I won't mind. We can take plenty of time getting used to each other."

I came to him, slid into his arms. "Don't be silly. Here I am, Mel—take me."

He was surprisingly gentle, carefully tender. He treated me as if I was something precious, a fragile, ethereal being who might shatter if he was at all clumsy. Mel was sweet and considerate, his practiced hands eliciting keyed responses from my taught body. We were together on the wide, soft couch, slow and understanding. For awhile.

I had him in me, and he moved slowly, strongly, with long, easy strokes that made ms shudder around him, that made me grip him with the sheath of my vagina. I was a hot, wet glove around his staff, a clenching of satiny muscles in this matchless intimacy of man and woman.

Mel was strong and sturdy. He knew the softly tantalizing places inside a woman, and he caressed them with his manhood, stroked them with his maleness, fondled them with the power of his organ.

I relaxed for him, allowed him to probe, to penetrate, to continue that steady, deep rhythm. It was good to lie almost passively, moving only my pelvis and buttocks in a sensuous acceptance of his strength and dominating maleness. It was good to be a complete female, to be used by this muscled, lusty man, to be a receptacle for his staff.

I was soft around him, clinging warmly and moistly to him, wriggling just enough so that I might give him more enjoyment, that he might feel my velvet caresses all along his organ. Lifting my hips, I invited him to plunge deeper. Arching my back, I begged him to bury himself in me.

The rocking movement was slow; it was a. cradle, an embrace of thighs and vagina and vulva, and legs and arms and the crushed mounds of my breasts. I was only for him; I was nothing for myself. I was the submissive woman, and he was the conquering man, and it was better this way, more fulfilling, more gratifying, more voluptuous.

But I felt the other thing coming, just as Mel Tani lurched and gasped in his first orgasm. I felt the surge of strength inside my thighs, and demand that I be the aggressor, that I move, attack, assault.

The now-familiar raging broke free inside me, and turned me into a primitive, clawing and shuddering. I tried to be all things to this man, to give. I succeeded only in reverting to the near-terrifying compulsion to master, to win, to be superior. And I fought Mel Tani as I had fought my other men, as I had battled fat and greedy Holcomb, as I had conquered Roy Warner.

Whatever the origin of this psychological quirk of mine—whether it resulted from the assaults of my step-father and step-brother or from the hate which filled me at being used by my ambitious husband to further his own cause—it would remain a part of my relationship with every man.

With the fury past, I expected punishment, rejection, unsatisfaction. But Mel Tani, in spite of his diamond-hard exterior, was like the others, underneath. He was only a man, shaken to his core by the savage violence of my love-making—shaken and smugly pleased that he had fanned such a devouring flame into life. A real man would have wanted my battle—but would have conquered me. But where was there a real man—a man completely stable and sure of himself?

Each time we were together, it was the same, two strong animals tearing at each other. Afterward, he was gentle again, solicitous, pampering me. No matter what Mel was to others, he was good to me. He protested when I decided I'd be a stripper. He didn't want other men's eyes clinging to my nude body. But I pointed out that they would only be looking. Anything else was strictly for Mel Tani alone.

I picked up the tricks of the trade from a full-blown, tired girl called Cindy. She'd been around the club circuits for years, and was on the verge of sliding all the way down. Cindy didn't kid herself, and she did her best to pass along what she had learned to me.

I got a kick out of stripping, from wiggling my hips within inches of staring, applauding men, from making obscenely suggestive bumps just out of their reach. I guess I was getting back at men in general, teasing them with a succulent prize they couldn't have, laughing at their sweaty frustrations.

Because I was young and tiny, the customers came back to watch. I grew to recognize many of the regulars, the goodtime charlies who'd ogly my gyrating body, then proposition one of the b-drinkers an hour later. Other faces became familiar, too—somber, watchful faces that didn't yell, that hovered above tables placed next to the wall. Some of these men would drift back to the office to talk with Mel; some of them left as quietly as they came.

I had no trouble with jerks grabbing for a free feel, no problems with characters slippily insistent about dating me later. The word was out. I was Mel Tani's girl, and the visiting firemen who didn't understand what that meant got tossed out on their ears.

So I thought it was Mel, when diffident knuckles rapped softly at my dressing room door one evening. I called, "Come in!"

And swung around on the makeup stool with a big grin. The grin faded when the man came hesitantly into the room and closed the door quickly behind him. It was Don Carson, my husband.

"L—Lee?"

"What the hell do you want? Long way from the sticks aren't you?"

He put out a shaky hand. He was thin, and the cuff of his shirt was frayed. "Don't be hard on me, Lee. I been a long time gettin' here. I might never have found you, if it wasn't for that picture outside—the one where you don't have anything on but a little—"

"I know," I said, and instinctively pulled my robe closer. "You still haven't told me what you want here."

Don rubbed a faintly bristled chin. He looked seedy. His hair was too long; there was a dark rim around his shirt collar. Don Carson didn't look like a backwoods dandy now. He looked exactly what he was—a cheap, lushing cornball a step or two away from skid row.

"Now, Lee; now, baby—I expect you're still my wife. And I came a hard way to find you, after I got fired. Just like that, they fired me, Lee. I didn't even know you was gone. I made that Roy Warner tell me where. You hear, I stood right up to him and made him tell me."

My lips curled. "A little late with your husbandly rights, weren't you?"

He was inching toward me, shuffling in the somehow plaintive, apologetic movement of the feet that drought-beaten sharecroppers use when they slide into the store to beg credit.

"I was purely wrong, Lee," he mumbled. "Roy Warner fixed it so I couldn't hire on anywhere in Mississippi. He blackballed me clean to Alabama. But I didn't care. All I wanted to do was find my little wife."

"Shut up," I said. "Just shut the hell up. I can imagine how you got out to the coast, and I know why you came. Okay—how much will take you out of town?"

Don blinked watery eyes. Close now, he smelled of boxcars and long dusty hours of plodding along baking highways while unheeding cars ignored his lifted thumb. I felt a twinge of something—guilt, regret, anger? I wasn't certain of my emotions. This pitiful imitation before me was my legal husband. And more than that—my rescuer, the strawhat knight with a shiny pistol who'd beaten back the dragons. More than that, even—Don was my first man ... I don't think any woman ever forgets her first.

"I—I need a place to stay, Lee. I need me a job, and clothes, and—"

"And a bottle," I finished. "Don't come any closer to me. You stink."

He hung his head. "Lee, Lee honey—"

I cursed him, spitting the harsh, cutting outhouse words into his cringing face. I told him what he had done to me with Mister Holcomb, how he had dilled something that might have grown into a flower. I told Don Carson just what a filthy, no-good, lousy man he was.

And do you know what he said? Can you imagine what that whining, gutless, country boy said? He said, "You're sure pretty when you're mad, Lee. Prettier'n I ever knew."

How the hell could I chase him out? My victory over Don had been complete from the moment he slunk in through the door like a whipped hound. But my transplanting from the piney woods had been too sudden, too complete. I should have known damned well that sound hounds will belly-crawl for a biscuit, then bite hell out of you when your back's turned.

I said, "Okay. Sit down over there and keep quiet. Mel—the boss doesn't like anybody in the dressing room. You were lucky to even make it back here. I'll go get some money for you. But Don—get this straight; get off my back, and stay off. I'll bring you enough to get you on your feet again, to hold you until you find a job. But this is it—it's final. I don't have a damned thing in common with you but your name, and that's sure as hell not tattooed on."

I stepped behind the screen to wriggle into a tight evening gown. I didn't want his eyes touching my flesh, but I could feel them sliding over my hips as I stalked out of the dressing room.

Mel was by the cash register. "I need about three hundred," I told him.

He didn't even frown. "Sure. That enough?"

The bills were crisp in my hand. "It had better be."

Mel touched my arm. "You know I don't care about the money. Anyone bothering you, making trouble? That's my department."

I managed a smile for him. "You're a sweet guy, Mel. Sweeter than I deserve. No, it's not really trouble. Not that kind. My husband showed up, beggin'. The real one, the one I told you I was separated from."

"You don't have to give him a dime." His eyes were dark and hard. "He won't ever come back, either. Just say the word."

I shook my head. "I—maybe I'm dippy, but I kind of feel sorry for him. He's a real nothing, but I feel sorry for him."

"Sure," Mel said. "Sure, you wouldn'be be Lee, if you weren't. Pay him off. What's it to us?"

"Nothing," I said and gave his strong hand a squeeze, "not a damned thing."

We were both wrong. Don took the money with shaking fingers, practically bowing and scraping in abject gratitude. As he crept out of the Club Tani with Mel's obsidian eyes following him, I thought I was done with Don Carson. I should have known better.

He was back within a week. I had just gone into my number, just shed the breakaway gown to the drumbeats and the clash of the cymbals, when I heard his voice bellowing from beyond the spotlight.

"Attagirl! Looka' there, ain't she pretty? My wife, th's who she is—my wife! You guys think that is all she is, huh? Just all frostin' without no good cake under it? Le' me tell you—that gal's just as good in bed—"

The blue spot held me pinned motionless in my black lace panties and the spangled pasties that just covered the tips of my breasts. The drummer picked up the beat to cover, but I didn't move. I just stood there, suddenly and inexplicably ashamed. All my book-thumping forebears loomed in the darkness beyond the floor, all the shalt-nots and brimstone.

I heard a glass shatter, the rising hum of voices, a chair leg banging against a table.

"Slut—tha's all she is—run off from her lawful man—"

Stiff-legged, I turned and headed for the security of the curtained alcove that led to the dressing rooms. The noise grew, echoing above the emcee's hurried patter. I sat before the makeup table and stared into the powder-flecked mirror. Damn him; damn him to the lowest depths of hell. One drunken voice from the past had stripped away my veneer of protection and left me helplessly naked again, turned me back to a scared, hungry kid. Damn Don Carson.

I cried until Mel put a hand on my shoulder, then I sat erect, dabbing at the tear-channeled makeup, trying to grin and not quite making it.

Mel's voice was soft. "The boys have him in the alley. I could have told you not to pay him off the first time. Slobs like that always come back for more. But I thought it was better to let you see it, let you make your own decision. What do you think now, Lee?"

What did I think? I never wanted to see that sweating red face again. I never wanted to hear that backwoods dialect again. Never. Never.

"Can—can you fix it, Mel? So he won't come back and bother me? I—I'll go to Reno, get a divorce; right away. Only I don't want to look at him again; I don't want to hear him again."

"I can fix it," Mel said. "Take the night off, Lee. Go home and wait for me."

I saw his eyes in the mirror. They weren't pretty. I felt a dark warning pushing at the back of my mind. The hell with it, I thought. Let Don find out about the efficiency of bouncers, let him know what it feels like to be badly beaten. He had it coming.

"See you later," I said to Mel.

Within an hour, he let himself into the apartment. I had a rosy glow on, and greeted him woozily from the bar. "Okay?"

"Sure," he said. "Nothing to worry about; all taken care of."

Bubbly with champagne and relief, I went to him. "Good. Now let me show you how grateful I am."

"That slob," he said. "That two-bit slob, embarrassing you like that."

"Forget it, Mel; I have. Honestly I have."

He looked down at me. "If you say so."

"Kiss me," I said, "and help me get out of this damned gown."

I made wild and aching love to Mel that night, trying perhaps to blot out the image of Don's face ground into the filth of the alley, the picture of heavy shoes slamming into Don's ribs. Mel's bouncers were tough and cold. They'd have done a thorough job.

That's what I thought had been done to Don, just a working-over, a brutal beating to impress upon that he musn't come back to the club. That's what I thought. Until the next afternoon, when I stretched yawning awake and began to read the paper over a cup of strong coffee.

The item was on page five, down near the bottom under a one-column head: "Visitor Drowns." The name seemed to leap out at me. I put down the coffee cup and looked again. It was still there.

"A man identified as Donald C. Carson of Mississippi was found off the beach this morning. The body was identified by a wallet the swimmer left on the beach with his towel and robe.

Police assume the drowned man took a taxi for an early morning swim, since no car was parked nearby."

Stunned, I read on. The coroner's report of accidental death by drowning, no marks on the body, lungs filled with water. It was just one of those things; regretable.

And neat. All the loose ends tied up. No further questions. The paper blurred as I shivered. I'd be willing to bet an arm that if the police looked for the cab driver, they'd have little trouble finding him. And I'd bet another arm that the hackie would swear he took this crazy character to the beach for a swim. It fitted together very well, very plausibly.

Except for one minor point. Don Carson couldn't swim.

CHAPTER EIGHT

Things speeded up after Don was "taken care of." Mel had to leave town twice within a month. The second time, he took me with him. And that time, I found out what brought the big money into his safety deposit box. It wasn't the Club Tani, although the place made better than expenses.

Mel did something with me that he'd probably never done in his life. He opened up to me, telling me everything, filling in the blanks in his background. I wasn't shocked. Maybe I have a part missing, lack some small emotional cog that other people have. I guess I stopped being shocked when my stepfather and stepbrother raped me, or when my husband forced me to accept another man in my bed. Maybe another woman would have stayed whole through all that. Well, I didn't.

Anyway, I calmly accepted the fact that Mel Tani was a professional gunman, a killer for hire. The idea excited me, made the insides of my thighs tingle and my breasts push against the confinement of my bra. Call it a morqid neurosis, a fringe sort of necrophilia; I can't look into myself and see exactly what makes me tick. Damned few people can.

I do know that the thought of conquering a man so ultimately, so finally, made me thrill, made me quiver. Such an act was complete power, utter mastery. Just move one finger, and the enemy was gone, snuffed out as if he never existed.

And it paid. I blinked when Mel told me how well it paid. I listened raptly as he went into details of his trade, what to avoid, what to look for, how to handle the weapons. He laughed aloud when I told him I already knew how to shoot, when I described the scene where I'd broken Pete Finney's kneecap and punched a hole through Jett Finney's scrawny stern.

Then he sobered. "Now it's all the way with us, Lee. Because it has to be. Did—did you ever think about, well,—about getting married again?"

He was a weird, sick combination, this man-killer and bashful boy. But he was good to Lee Carson. That was all that mattered.

"Yes," I said, "I've thought about it. But I didn't want you to feel you had to tie me to you that way. You don't have to, now. I can keep my mouth shut, Mel."

His eyes held mine. "I know that. If I didn't you'd have been out on the street a long time ago. Only that's not what I mean, Lee. It's different with you and me. We fit together. You're strong and I'm strong. Together we're unbeatable."

"Right," I said. If you call what we had strength.

"You haven't answered me. I asked you to marry me, Lee."

"I thought you knew the answer. Sure."

He held me close. "After the next contract. We can make it a honeymoon trip. New Orleans is a great town. We can do it up brown."

"Yeah, like newlyweds."

I never got to know the feeling of being legally married to Mel Tani, although I don't think an official piece of paper could have brought us any closer together. After, it didn't matter.

I remember Mel was like a kid on the plane, livelier than I had ever seen him; jumpier, too. I reminded him of how we'd met on a plane, and he said something about fate. Then his mood changed, darkening. With his lips hidden in my hair, he whispered that there was plenty of money, that a guy couldn't go on pushing his luck for the Combine, that filling this contract should be the last one. He had me, now. He never worried about a contract before, but now he had me to look after.

When Mel slept at last, I frowned into the unseen clouds outside the window. The last hour or so hadn't sounded like Mel Tani at all. I wondered if I was good for him. I thought of the black notebook in my purse, the one with the contract-maker's phone number in it, and other numbers and addresses in L.A. and San Francisco. Mel said it would be safer with me until after the hit; just in case.

He was right about that. Without the book and the key to Mel's deposit box, Lee Carson would have been in a hell of a mess, after what happened in New Orleans. As it was, that town still has the ring of bad luck to me. The Combine thinks I have a pet superstition about New Orleans, because I've always refused to make a hit there. The Combine is right. I don't want a damned thing to do with that Cliptown on the river.

We got in just as the city was lighting up for the night. It looked pretty, all lights and water. It even smelled different—cape jasmine and magnolias. The hotel Mel picked wasn't the biggest nor the best, but its rooms were clean and quiet, and there was no house detective. It's a damned good thing Mel was so careful, as it worked out.

I was waiting in the room for him to come back. He'd already worked out the details, basing his plan on the concise information furnished on the target's habits. Mel knew exactly where this guy would be, at any hour. He. knew where to make the hit so it would be smooth and almost unseen. Mel was a real pro.

But even professionals slip up, and in this business you're only allowed one mistake. Thinking back, I guess Mel had too much on his mind; he was too tied up emotionally with me and his plans for our future together. Our future was damned short.

A soft, muffled thump on the hotel room door made me whirl from the window. It came again. I stood close to the panel and said, "Mel?"

"In," he grunted. "Let me in, Lee."

He collapsed on the bed. Blood was bright over the hand clenched against his chest. Mel's face was pale, his eyes full of pain.

"Loused it up," he mumbled as I took away the hand and stuffed a towel across the hole in his body. "Loused it up ... only nicked him. He—he got me from his knees. Who—who coulda' figured that Wop to shoot so good."

"Mel," I said, "Mel—"

He closed his eyes. "Gun in my pocket ... get—get rid of it ... and get out, Lee. Get out of this town."

"NO—I'll call a doctor, pay him big so—"

His eyes fluttered open. "Don't act like a hick. You can't pay big enough to keep a doc quiet and—and I don't think one could help. Take—take the key, but get—get rid of the book. Burn it. Throw the gun into the river ... get the plane back. The key—money's all yours, Lee. Take it and run. One good thing I'll ever do. Guys—guys are gonna' be asking questions, they're gonna' be after the money. Run, Lee ... run."

Trembling, I stared down at him. "The contract—the man who hired you; he can help. I'll call him, make him come."

Mel tried to laugh. The effort turned his lips red. He gasped for air. "N—no, baby. He finds me, I'm dead quicker, that's—that's all. And one name in the book, you forget you ever saw. Bailey—you forget you ever heard of Bailey. Lee—"

"Yes," I said, but there wasn't any more. I leaned down and put my ear to his chest. He wasn't dead. I didn't know how much longer he would live, though.

I took the gun, dropped it into my purse. I slid Mel's wallet out of his pants, took his ring and watch. Not for the money, for the things themselves. He'd told me cops can make identification from little leads. And if the New Orleans cops pegged Mel, they'd soon be sweating me.

Down the back stairs, I struggled with both our suitcases, not daring to leave either of them behind. A block over, the shabby street was lined with cheap ginmills; a derelict lay sprawled in the gutter.

I couldn't have picked a better spot. I placed Mel's suitcase on the corner. By the looks of the neighborhood, it would disappear the minute I walked away.

Two more blocks and I flagged a cab, rode it to the train station. Out of the terminal's other door, I got into another taxi, directed the driver to the airport, and settled back to think. I wasn't doing badly so far, but it had been mostly instinct and the desire to survive. I had no illusions about Mel's playmates. They wouldn't want me around.

I thought over a lot of angles before I got out of the cab. Checking my suitcase through to Phoenix instead of L.A. seemed a good idea. I'd ticket myself there, switch over to a non-scheduled line the rest of the way. Just in case.

Then I had another idea. I didn't know how much money Mel had stashed away in that bank box, but I didn't think it would last me the rest of my life. I was going to need a job, and I had just the business in mind. As for Mel—a sweet guy, in his way. But dying now in a deserted room. I couldn't help him; nobody could. I could help myself. I made the call from a quiet booth, the black notebook before me. A man answered the ring, "Yeah?"

I said it fast, "You want Mel Tani. Room 306, Hotel Conti. He's still alive."

Silence, then, "Yeah? Who are you?"

"A woman. Just remember that—a woman called you. You don't have to worry. Mel is unconscious."

"Listen, girlie—"

I hung up. The man would remember all right. I said a little goodbye to Mel as I got on the plane for Phoenix. It wasn't as if I'd sold him out. It was just good business now. He was dying anyway. If the contract man didn't silence him for keeps, the cops might find him and take down notes from his delirium.

Before the plane was halfway to Arizona, I was asleep. Only one of the dreams bothered me. I remembered that never once had I told Mel I loved him; never once had he said the words to me. It was just as well.

When I got back to Los Angeles, I went to the address penned under one name in the book. Mel's last words to me had been to forget I ever heard of Bailey. That meant Bailey was the number one boy on this part of the coast, the big man of the Combine. Forget him, hell. He was the guy I wanted to see.

The office looked legitimate. Two typists banging away, a little bald character at the water fountain. I stopped by one of the typists. "Mr. Bailey, please."

She had bulging eyes behind thick glasses. "Do you have an appointment?"

"Tell him I just got back in town. From New Orleans."

"Oh; I—I don't know—"

There was a box on her desk, one of those inter-office gadgets. I hit all the switches with my palm. "Mister Bailey—I brought you a souvenir. From New Orleans."

The box grunted. "Send the young lady in, Miss Pringle."

Miss Pringle wiped her glasses and gave me a little jerk of the head. I went into Bailey's office.

He didn't look like I'd pictured him. He was almost bald, and his paunch bulged over the desk edge. But when I saw his eyes, that was something else. I've seen swamp rattlers who looked gentler. I walked over to him slowly, rolling my hips, lifting my breasts, smiling a little.

"There's plenty of that down the street," Bailey said. "For five bucks a throw. You got in here, miss. Where's the—souvenir?"

I unsnapped my purse. "Right here," I said. "Keep your hand on the desk."

He sat very still, waiting, those icy eyes unblinking. Keeping the muzzle of Mel's .38 steady, I came around the desk and snapped the cold mouth of the gun hard into his ear.

"What are the odds," I murmured, "that if you jump, you get your brains scrambled?"

Bailey let his breath hiss from between set teeth. "The odds are too long. I'm not bucking them. Say what you want."

I didn't relax the pressure of the muzzle. "I say Mel Tani; if that's not the magic name, how about New Orleans; How about Pietro Agnelli?"

"I know you," he said. "Mel's girl. The stripper."

"Ex-stripper," I corrected. "I have another job in mind."

"I'm not the damned fool Mel was," Bailey said. "There's no money here—not the kind you want, anyway."

"Mel was stupid," I said. "He just got careless. I don't want money, Bailey. No more than I can earn. As Mel's replacement."

He stiffened. "You're kidding."

I shoved the gun barrel. "Does it feel like it?"

"Be—be careful of that thing. If that's Tani's gun—"

"It is. And I realize it has a hair trigger."

He waited. I waited. Then he said: "You know Tani got it?"

"I know who got him, too," I said. "Agnelli. I called Agnelli."

"You—you called Agnelli? After Tani was—"

"Useless, dying. Better Agnelli than the cops."

Bailey thought that over. "Okay," he said. "You made a point. Take that rod out of my ear."

I backed up. "Do I get Mel's job?"

Carefully, he fingered sweat away from his forehead. "So you put on a good act; you walked in here and put a gun on me. That don't make you a hitter. And as for fingering your boyfriend—"

"To the right party. Check Agnelli. He'll tell you a woman called him. Who else but me? Listen, Bailey—I got to you, didn't I? Men don't suspect a woman so quickly. Look at me—don't you think I couldn't attract a target?"

"That," Bailey said, "you get no argument on. Only—"

"Only can I shoot? I'm a hillbilly; I've had to make one lousy 22 shell do for a meal. If I missed, I didn't eat. I ate. As for proving I've got guts enough to cut down a man—well, you thought so. I'll just have to show you, if you'll give me a chance."

He looked at me for a long time. Then, "You know, I believe you would kill a man—with no more compunction than your boyfriend had. You're pretty smart; you came to me, instead of selling Tani's black book to the cops, or to some other guys. Like you said, I don't know how you'll do when the chips are down. But what the hell can I lose? You miss, somebody else don't. Somebody else don't miss you, either! You know that?"

"I know," I said, putting the 38 back into my purse and standing erect. I smoothed the dress over my hips. "But that crack about the five-buck stuff on the street—I don't come cheap, Bailey. Tell me, do you want me to demonstrate how much I'm worth—that way?"

He shook his head. "Your lover cold in the market, a rod in your purse, ice in your veins. No thanks. I'd rather make out with a black widow spider. I know where to reach you. But for business, widow—just for business."

When I left Bailey's office, I had my nickname—The Widow. I had something else, the job I wanted. Mel Tani had a replacement. All I had to do was show the Combine I was as good as he had been.

I had other stops to make—the bank, where Mel's pass key would let me check on the money I had. Then to the club, to let Mel's manager know where I could be reached. Then where? Shopping, maybe. I had several articles in mind, and not all of them were new clothes.

I was a damned fool. I was an unthinking, clumsy idiot. The last place in the world I should have shown my face was the Club Tani. Caught up in new and exciting plans, moving so fast I didn't have time to plan, I walked myself right into it.

The club manager gave a quick get-outa'-here nod, but the two guys at the bar caught it and closed in on me. The tall one said, "Miss Carson?"

"Y—yes. What—"

The short guy took my purse.

"Hey—" I said.

"Cute," the short guy said. "A 38 special. Nice toy."

I closed my mouth, and kept it that way.

"Your fingerprint was cute, too," the tall cop said. "The red one you left on the hotel towel. Goody for us that nightclub entertainers in so many states have to be printed, isn't it?"

"Yeah," I said, "Goody for you. There's something else in that purse, shorty—and it's counted to the penny."

He grinned at me. "It might buy you a good lawyer. You need one."

If I hadn't been flip, they might have left off the handcuffs. It was an uncomfortable ride with them on. I knew they couldn't pin Mel's killing on me; that hole in his chest had been too big for a 38. But there were other raps—unlawful flight, withholding evidence, carrying concealed weapon, etc.,etc. Those little etc.'s could get me some time in a place I didn't want to see. They did.

But everything happens for the best. I realize now that Bailey wouldn't have used me just on a gun-act and my say-so. In fact, some messy accident might have picked me to happen to. Something like a drowning in the bay.

Going to prison with my mouth still tightly shut proved me to the Combine. They knew I could have copped out, or at least made things unhappy for a few of them. I saw to it that word got back to them about the black book, that I'd tucked it into the deposit box. And they must have gotten a laugh out of what I did with the key to that box. I didn't—I had a hell of a time rescuing that key from the bathroom, later. Sure I swallowed it. I didn't figure they'd bother to x-ray—not after the probing shakedown the police matron gave me.

And in the "joint" I picked up a lot of know-how that was going to help me when I got out. Two years is a cheap price to pay for all I learned, because I was going to be drawing returns for those years for a long, long time to come.

As The Widow, trusted gunner for the Conbine.

CHAPTER NINE

In California, "prison" is a dirty word. The authorities prefer to call their penal establishments "correctional facilities." As if that made any difference. A jail is a joint, and pretty words won't change that.

Joints are divided into three classifications—maximum security, medium security, and minimum. Which means you'll play hell breaking out of the first kind, the odds are lower on the second, and you can just walk away from the minimum security joints.

For a few miles. Then you're picked up and slapped back into the maximum joint, because you're an escape artist now, and you'll do the extra time for it. Maybe not officially, but the parole board will be damned sure you get "shot down" the next few times you come up before it. Shot down is prison slang for parole denied.

But if you're a good girl and stay out of trouble, if you "mam" hell out of the matrons and cooperate with the sociologists and psychologists, you may not even have to sweat out a parole. You can go out without the"tail," without the probationary period of so many years, so many months. On a straight release, you're free and clean. No parole officer on your back, no ordinary citizen's privileges denied.

Straight releases aren't common, except with a few first offenders. Even though it was my first fall, I'd have played hell coming out clean if I hadn't had help on the outside. I made it, but first I did a full two years behind bars in a maximum joint that I won't name now. Too many people might remember me, even with all the camouflage I'm using.

It wasn't fun. Being penned in never is. I think the worst part is being completely cut off from a normal sex life. And the loneliness that hangs like grey fog over the repetition of one day just like the other.

I guess the officials try. California joints are called country clubs by cons who've done hard time in other states. There are movies, hobby shops, plenty of reading material, educational classes of all kinds. And the counseling classes. I musn't forget those. But no matter how it's dressed, any length of time away from the outside world is still plain hell.

Prisons have caste systems. At the top are the girls with protection of a sort, the murderers, those who were involved in bank stickups, and check artists. The scale goes down, through shoplifters and car thieves, down more to include petty crooks and dope pushers. At the very bottom are the sex offenders, and I don't mean prostitutes and the average lesbians. They're accepted, all right, because every girl behind walls has prostituted herself in one way or another. But the bottom of the scale women, harassed and pushed at every turn, are the sexually twisted who have been caught with minors. These women do hard time, reviled and mistreated and sometimes killed.

The headshrinkers may have fancier terms for this, but I think it's because some of the inmates have young sons and daughters outside, and it enrages them to picture their own being jammed up by some sly wench. Given any excuse or semblance of one, they'll beat hell out of the sex offenders. Of course, their own sex lives are warped, but that doesn't count. The circumstances are different.

I looked like fresh meat when the big gates swung shut behind me. Tiny and young, I was target for a hundred pairs of smouldering eyes as I went through the admission routine. But I was still too damned mad at my own stupidity to be afriad. I wasn't like the rest of these plain, grey women. When they put their hands on me, they'd find that out.

But without attention-getting violence. I sure as hell didn't want to call official attention to Lee Carson. Repeatedly, my lawyer had drummed that into my head—stay out of trouble, keep quiet. For that, he got four or five thousand I'd had in my purse when I was picked up. He didn't earn it in court. All he did there was plead me guilty, and make a speech about my youth, bad companions and my first offense.

There were too many women on the jury. I knew I was dead when I saw them checking my shape, my showgirl-length hair, and my unconsciously suggestive walk. Besides, there never was much chance of beating the rap. That fingerprint on the towel in Mel's blood, his gun, the five gees I had. All the evidence said guilty, and that's the verdict the jury brought in. I didn't blame them. I blamed myself for getting caught.

The Combine watched me, from the time I went into court, and right up to the prison walls. I knew they'd continue keeping an eye on me inside. If I showed signs of cracking, of being ready to try for a deal to get my time shortened, some quiet girl would ambush me in some dark hall and leave me there in my own blood. The Combine has methods of reaching people inside the joints—a big bundle deposited in a trust fund for some lifer's kids, a warning of a son or husband put under a gun, cute methods like that. They get results.

So I had to walk easy and stay clammed up. That didn't mean I had to submit to lecherous pawings from mannish women; it didn't mean I'd be forced to take any dirty work these broads wanted to dish out. Just the opposite. If I wanted to do quiet, easy time, I'd better establish myself quickly.

There was a snap job waiting for me, a paid-for cop tossed my way by the Conbine. Being a library assistant suited me fine. I'd have the knowledge of the world at my fingertips, and the girls would know I had strings pulled for me on the outside. My rap sheet worked for me, too, automatically placing me in the higher echelons if inmate society. I'd been missed up in a murder, carrying a gun when the law nailed me. That made me someone to watch, a tough girl.

Only there are a few women in joints who don't give a damn what you are, or who's behind you. These are the borderline psychotics, the lesbians, the women who've made their own world inside the walls. These were the ones I had to worry about.

The headshrinker warned me about them, being chummy and all-wise during the interview all newcomers must sit through. I didn't react the way she wanted; I didn't tremble and beg for help. Instead, I stared calmly back at the woman's thick glasses, waiting. Otherwise, I cooperated, answering all her sly questions truthfully—or almost so.

Doctor Asbury made doodles on her notebook, and frowned at me. "Lee," she said, first-naming to show she was my friend, "Lee, there's something about you that puzzles me. Your tests show a high degree of intelligence and aptitude, in spite of your lack of formal education. But I sense another Lee Carson, a girl hidden away. That other girl is almost frightening; cold, callous, uncaring, with a conscience."

I smiled. "Oh, come now, Doctor—I thought extra-sensory perception was still in the science fiction stage, or at best, only experimental."

She didn't smile back. "It's not ESP. Part of it shows in your word-association tests, in your Rorshach responses. I'd be tempted to list you as a narcissist, Lee—someone who is in love with herself; or perhaps a hedonist—a pleasure-seeker. But there are overlapping emotions, or the lack of same. There's a frightening quality about you."

I managed to laugh. "In here, doctor? Besides, my record jacket doesn't carry me as a murderer, or anything like that."

"No," Doctor Asbury said thoughtfully, "not yet."

The hell with her. I had cooperated, and I'd continue to do so. Up to a point. Just as I'd cooperate with anything else the prison big wheels wanted me to do. I wanted out, and being a "model" inmate was the quickest way through the gate.

Ten days later, I ran into my first trouble. Marcie Wilks was big, burly, and doing time on an ADW rap—assault with a deadly weapon; a long, sharp knife. She'd cut up her girl friend in a jealous fit of rage. She wore her hair short and walked with a swagger. She was my roommate. One look at Marcie, and I knew damned well she'd make a pass, sooner or later. I didn't want trouble with her, but neither did I want to be her girl. I had to take my chances and trust to the con's code of silence.

I stood quietly as she finally clamped one big hand on my buttocks and squeezed. "Firm," she whispered, "velvet, but firm."

"I'm like that all over," I said, with a quick glance at the by-rules open door.

"Don't fret," Marcie said. "The matron just made her rounds. She won't be back until lights-out. Nobody else will bother us, either. I've seen to that."

"Got it all planned, Marcie?"

Her hand was still kneading my haunch. "Sure; that's the way I work. The matron don't expect it with the lights on. I'm going to give you a break, Lee—a real break."

"Yeah," I said, and casually moved from under her hand. She was leaning forward, legs wide in a mannish stance. I set both feet and drove one balled fist hard into her lower groin, the other into a sagging breast.

Marcie wasn't expecting it. She gasped, clutching in agonized reflex at herself. I moved silently in and backhanded a vicious chop across her exposed throat. I'd learned that little trick from watching the bouncers operate at the Club Tani. The blow takes all the guts out of a trouble maker. Marcie's face purpled as she fell backward across her cot. Her heavy legs jerked spasmodically.

I looked at the door again, then put a knee into her heaving belly and leaned down to get a good grip on both sides of her head. My thumbs were hooked, their nails barely touching Marcie's fluttering eyelids.

"Hear me well, Marcie," I said. "I can take your eyes out right now, if that's the way you want it. Or I can rip them out at any time in the future. Like this."

I pressed down gently, feeling her eyeballs give slightly under my nails. Marcie felt it, too. She was still fighting to suck air through her bruised throat, still writing from the shock of my punches to her breast and belly.

"P—please—" she croaked.

I got off her, went over to sit on my own bed and watch as she slowly recovered. Marcie's eyes were murderous when she muttered, "Damn you."

I shrugged. "Just so we understand each other."

She massaged her throat, fingered her eyes. "Okay—okay; you're new here, and it's your first rap. You don't know how it's going to be; you don't know how many nights you're going to lie awake and run your thighs together and pant for a man. Only there are no men here."

"I'll make out," I said.

"You think. Give it a little time, and that won't satisfy you, either. You'll think you're going crazy; you'll dream wild things and you'll wake up crying. Go ahead, Lee—be tough now. You'll come to me, or to someone like me, and you'll beg. You hear me, tough girl—you'll beg!"

"Shut up," I said. "Shut the hell up before I decide solitary and losing a chance at the parole board wouldn't be so bad."

"Sure," Marcie grunted. "I don't have to push it. I've got time; I've got plenty of time. And so have you."

The hell of it was, she was right. About everything—the night sweats, the erotic dreams, the tension building until you felt it had to explode. Marcie was right about everything—except I didn't beg. I didn't say a damned thing when she came to me many months later. Maybe I whimpered when she came into my bed and coiled around me, but that was all.

She was warm and she knew what she was doing to me, and I just didn't seem to give a damn that she was a lesbian; I didn't care that she was a woman, and that somehow it was wrong for one woman to make love to another. I needed; I ached, I hurt all over because I had been cut off from sexual gratification, except the kind I could give myself. So I accepted Marcie for what she was, and for what she was making of me.

Marcie kissed me; she crushed her mouth on mine and forced my lips apart so she could dart her tongue between my teeth and find my own tongue to caress wetly and hotly. Her breath hissed into my mouth, and I found my own breath panting agreement.

Her hands were all over me, cupping and squeezing my breasts, sliding over my back and hips and belly. Her mouth left mine and dipped swiftly to my breasts; she kissed them and fondled them, then sucked and rolled the nipples between her teeth, pulling upon them as I squirmed and clung to her.

Her head went lower, down over the taug skin of my heaving rib cage, to my belly and its dimple, to my hips and my groin and—oh, oh—Marcie was what I wanted and what I needed, and her mouth, her lips, her tongue and her teeth were so deft, so practiced. She did things to me that no man had ever been able to do; she teased every erogenous spot, stimulated every touch zone, and when she began work upon my aching clitoris, I almost went out of my mind.

It was wild and wet and wonderful. I locked my thighs about her adorable head and squeezed her deeper into me. I swung my hips and hunched my pelvis and fed myself to her, wanting her to hurt me and devour me. She caressed and clenched the muscles of my buttocks as she made lesbian love to me, and I remember rolling my head helplessly from side to side and moaning softly as I reached a mighty, ripping orgasm that shook us both.

CHAPTER TEN

Doing a "fall" can make or break you. It didn't break me. I listened to the oldtimers, to con angles and to plans the girls had for their futures. Most of those plans would never work out, and the planners would be right back inside for their second fall, and their third, until their dreams would seem impossible fantasies even to the dreamers.

But some of the talk helped me—a careless word here, a name dropped there; contacts and rackets and cops on the take; pimps and pusher and heister. I had a tidy file of information tucked away inside my head when I went up before the board that would either set my time or "shoot me down"—postpone my hearing until the following year.

I'd been a good girl: helpful, studious, attentive. And I hadn't done a damned thing to make the still-listening Combine suspicious of me. I was hopeful that the word had been passed, that somebody on the board could be reached.

I don't know which did it—my spotless record as an inmate, or a payoff. But I walked out of the board room with weak knees and damp eyes as the reaction set in. In just three weeks, I was slated to leave prison, and with the coveted "no-strings" release in my purse.

The last night came around and I couldn't sleep a wink. I sat smoking one cigarette after another, jittery, anxious.

Marcie Wilks said: "Lee?"

LEE CARSON

"No," I answered into the dark. "Not any more; not ever again."

"Maybe," she murmured from her bed. "Just maybe. I've seen it happen before. After you've been inside, after you've been with—me, you might not find men so attractive any more."

"Not me," I said. "It was temporary and it's over. Now I want a man. I want a man so damned bad that my belly hurts. and I'll have one tomorrow night. Just as soon as I can find a room, I'll find a man."

The air outside was different, clean, stimulating. Without looking back, I walked quickly away from the big walls and down the street toward the taxi stand. A faint, knowing leer was pasted on the hackie's face as I carried my suitcase to the curb. I guess he enjoyed feeling superior to the girls who came across that particular stretch of sidewalk, and maybe he was conscious of the need emanating from us, a palpable sexuality that made us almost helpless at the presence of a man.

Not this one, I decided. Not this grinning ape smelling of plastic seat covers and cheap shaving lotion. I could wait. I'd already waited two years.

I didn't have to get into his cab. A man drifted close and touched my elbow. "Bailey," he said.

The cabbie frowned. "Look, Mac—"

The other man ignored him. "My car's around the corner."

"Fine," I said. "I hoped someone would meet me."

"Look," the cabbie said again.

Bailey's man turned slowly and did just that. He looked, not saying anything, standing quietly. The cabbie saw something that made his face turn pale. He swallowed and shuffled back to his call phone.

In the car, my thigh brushed his and sent a quiver racing through me. My hands shook as I fumbled in my purse for a cigarette. My fingers touched the lipstick tube, and I held the smooth metal for a moment. After I brought the safety deposit key out of a hiding place that had defied a dozen surprise shake-downs by the matrons, it had taken me anxious hours to center it inside the soft red stuff, to make the lipstick perfectly round and innocent.

The man didn't look at me. His plain, undistinguished face stared straight ahead as he maneuvered the car through growing traffic, "I know how you must feel," he said, "and I'd like to help. But Bailey says no. You have a job to do."

I choked on cigarette smoke. "A—j—job? Right now?"

He nodded, reached into his coat and slid an envelope across the seat. "It's all in there. After you memorize the information, burn the paper."

Five hundred dollars, a car key, a list of addresses and times, a snapshot, and a name: Johnny Malloy.

"Three days," my driver said. "Bailey's in a hurry. Your car's in that lot over there, the grey Plymouth. A gun's clipped under the dash."

Turning, he really stared at me for the first time. "Damned shame Bailey's in such a hurry," he said. "I envy Johnny Malloy. Partly, that is."

"And afterward?" I asked.

"See you in L.A. The YMCA."

I had to laugh. I was still grinning when I put my suitcase into the grey Plymouth and slid behind its wheel. Then I realized the guy hadn't even told me his name. That wasn't too important, and at the moment, neither was the compulsion to lie naked and loved in some man's arms. That drive was being overridden by something stronger, the need to prove myself to Bailey, to make a success out of my first assignment. And I didn't kid myself. I wanted to kill this Johnny Malloy. Or any other man.

Men had driven me out of my childhood home; men had bargained over me as if I was a tasty bit of mindless meat; men had taken me and ogled me, and made me a present of two years behind bars. From now on, it was going to be my turn.

When I was heading north on the freeway, the car pointed for the city of San Francisco, I reached a tentative hand below the dash. My fingers found the butt of the pistol. I stroked the checkered grip, feeling the latent power it held, the power of life and death that needed only my whim to release its mighty thunder.

I left the car at a filling station in the suburbs, as I'd been instructed. A taciturn mechanic drove me into the heart of town. From there, I caught a taxi to the best hotel and checked in as Mrs. Joyce Markham of Seattle. In the mezzanine shops, I spent three hundred dollars on an evening dress and two severely tailored suits.

In my room, I memorized Johnny Malloy's habits, stamped the features of his face indelibly upon my mind. The pistol was in my purse, and I saw that its silencer was the same kind that Mel Tani had used, its cylinder full of shiny .38 cartridges. I thought back to something Mel told me: work close and put it in the body; the torso is a big target.

That didn't worry me. I didn't doubt my ability to put a bullet where I wanted it to go. That part was easy. But I wondered briefly if I'd freeze at the wrong moment, if I'd get buck fever and miss an opportunity that might never come again.

It would be too damned bad for me, if I did. If Johnny Malloy didn't get me, Bailey would. Not personally, of course. He'd just give another envelope to someone, and Lee Carson would be the target, a failure to be wiped off the books of a business that couldn't condone failure.

I studied the list of places Malloy was apt to be. He was a fight fan, and the newspapers carried a story of boxing matches at the

Cow Palace. Ergo, Johnny Malloy ought to be at ringside. It cost me another fifty dollars—twenty for a pair of seats, thirty more to be certain the seats were next to Malloy's usual reservations.

Three days, Bailey had given me. I'd better tie up the hit by then, because I was already short of expense money, and I was a long way from the bank box in L.A. The thousand I'd had in my account when I went to jail; Spent over the two years, for small bribes, canteen luxuries, in buying my way into the good graces of matrons and cops alike.

The Cow Palace is a huge echoing cavern, its upper decks stretching into darkness. Most of the fight bugs were already buzzing expectantly when I was guided to my seat. Two seats, rather; but nobody would occupy the other. That was reserved for my "escort"—a wraith who would never materialize. Its emptiness would separate me from Johnny Malloy.

Out of the corner of my eye, I saw him come into the row, a big, cheery man with a freckled face and red hair. Two quiet men followed him, their eyes flicking over me and the empty seat, then going on to search the other faces. Malloy glanced at me and settled back to watch the first fight. The preliminary was a slow one, making it easy for me to draw attention by shifting nervously, checking my watch, looking back at the aisle. Obviously, I was a woman being stood up, and concerned about it.

My tailored suit marked me as no fight-mob girl, its cunningly draped materials clinging to my body in a calculated blending of sensuousness and good taste. I sighed and took deep fretful breaths, lifting my breasts against the translucent blouse. It wasn't difficult to pretend agitation. Every movement of my body reminded me that I had been away from men for a long time. Too damned long.

The semi-final bout gave me my chance. The fight was bloody, a battle of punchers, and I acted out my role. Flinching, I looked away from the ring, fumbled in my purse for a handkerchief. Swaying, I held the bit of perfumed cloth to my mouth, peering through my lowered lashes to see if Malloy had noticed. He had. I started a slow slide out of my seat, tumbling loosely forward in a pretty good imitation of a faint.

Cornball? You wouldn't think it, to see Johnny Malloy jump sideways to catch me before I hit the floor. He lifted me easily, ignoring the yells behind us. My head lolled, my arms dangled. I kept my eyes closed until we were out of the crowd at ringside. I opened them weakly and pushed against his chest.

"P—please—"

"It's okay, lady," he rumbled. "You fainted. You'll be all right in a minute. The guy oughta' be whipped for standing up a lady like you, when you're not used to seeing fights."

"G—guy? Oh—Harry—I suppose he was delayed somehow. If you don't mind, I think I can stand up now. I do thank you, mister—"

"Malloy," he grinned, "Johnny Mallory."

It was easy as that. Bewildered, grateful, I allowed myself to be talked into a drink to settle my nerves. In a quiet and respectable hotel bar, of course. Malloy was pleased with himself, acting the part of the gallant. I said things about how terrible it was for men to hurt each other, and over my second martini, mentioned that San Francisco was so much more romantic than Seattle. My missing escort Harry? A business acquaintance of my husband's, something to do with lumber. I admitted I was upset by Harry. Enough to have a third drink, thank you.

I didn't have to fake the effect those martinis were having. After two dry years, they were warm bombs in my body. Johnny's face got fuzzy around the edges. But I could still see the casual jerk of the head that dismissed the bodyguards hovering in the background at another table. Half-heartedly, I protested that he'd done too much for me already, that he needn't see me back to my hotel. All the while, I felt his eyes sliding over the front of my blouse, felt the tentative brushing of his knee against my nylons.

In the taxi, I struggled properly before allowing his mouth to close over mine. His made me dizzier than the liquor had. For a moment, I melted to him submissively, wanting nothing more than his hands on my body, not remembering anything except his nearness and his maleness.

I had to tear myself away from his caress. The wobble in my legs as he helped me into the lobby wasn't all make-believe. With an effort, I walked sedately past the desk and into the elevator with Johnny cupping my elbow. The clerk pretended he didn't see. They never do, when the guests wear expensive suits bought from the shop across the lobby.

I let us into my second-floor room, pawing convincingly at the light switch. "Whoops," I said. "I'm sort of groggy. My-my husband doesn't like me to drink. I get so silly. If he knew—"

"Seattle is far away," Johnny said huskily. "How can he know?"

Swaying, I blinked at him. "That's right. Since his old friend Harry stood me up, how can he know?"

This time, when Johnny pressed me close, I felt the bulge of the shoulder holster. I pretended not to notice, giving myself wholly up to his searching kiss. It shook me to my toes, set the long-held forces to boiling within me. Helplessly, I writhed against him, my hands locked around his head, lifting my body on tiptoe. A warning buzzed in the back of my mind. Not too eagerly, I thought. Act it out, play coy.

I pulled away, eyes wide, lips quivering. "N—no; please-no. I'm not one of those—Johnny, you've been very nice to me. But I'm frightened; I didn't mean anything like this—"

He reached for me again. "But I did, Joyce. From the minute I saw you falling out of that seat, from the minute I carried you so soft and helpless away from the ring. Don't tell me to go away. Not now. I know you're not a cheap pickup. I could tell you were class, right away. Don't tell me to go away, Joyce."

I put one hand to my mouth. "I—I don't know. There's something fascinating about you, Johnny—a strength and power I've never had."

He waited, not pushing things, his big hands lightly on my waist. A half-sob pushed itself from my mouth. "Be—be—be good to me, Johnny."

Malloy swept me into his arms and carried me to the bed. As he lowered me upon it, I murmured, "The lights, Johnny—please, the lights."

When he went grinning to flip the switch, I looked quickly at the partially open bathroom door. The .38 was in there, folded in a towel and balanced atop the shower stall. It could wait. I Wanted Johnny Malloy alive for awhile

In the frenzied time that followed, I barely hung onto my image as a straying wife overpowered by the irresistible virility of a rare and potent lover. I wanted to unclench my teeth and let the muddy, hissing words pour over him. I wanted to tell him what to do to me, and how to do it. Instead, I let my body speak for me. Johnny Malloy must have been surprised by the savagery he unleashed when he brought me to him.

We fell over onto the bed, and my nyloned legs thrashed wildly for a moment, showing the lace panties, the fullness of my thighs. He held me closely, kissing me hard, running his tongue into my mouth. I pressed to him and kissed him back, but I couldn't make myself play the lady any longer. I wasn't a lady, but a hot, wild bitch in heat, at last out of the kennels and rubbing against a male.

I slipped out of my dress, wanting to rip it away, but warned by a small part of my brain that I'd need it again soon. I whipped off undies and bared myself to this eager man, who was already as naked as me. I bit his throat and his upper chest. I took his nipple into my teeth and worried it like a dog; I raked his back with my fingernails and ground my pelvis, my pubic hair, into him, glad that he was built big and swollen and long, glad that he was a bull, a stud, a man.

Taking his organ with one hand, I fed it into myself as I lifted a leg over him and hunched close. I was gasping and squirming and going insane, and the first touch of that soft-hard head, flanged and slitted, made my brain whirl. I humped and took him swiftly, completely into me. Oh, it was good. It was wonderful. It was hard and round and long, and it moved into my vagina and I swear to the entrance of my womb and against my clitoris and my vulva grasped at it in eager desperation.

I moaned and tossed as he stroked it into me. I heaved and twisted, and clawed and cried big rolling tears. I bucked and gyrated upon his dear, darling rod, and when he came the first time, I wouldn't even let him slow up. I continued to roll and twist upon him, to fondle his sac in my fingers as my sheath fondled his organ. I hit an orgasm and hit again, cried out in ecstasy and pumped away for another one. My lover was shocked at my furious attack, and I could feel the wonder in him.

I didn't give him time to wonder. Every inch of my flesh demanding and violent; I took him as. I took all men—viciously, my hands running wildly over him. Johnny was a big man and strong, but the stunning releases of passions too-long withheld geysered through me. It was over too soon, too soon. Limply, I fell away from him, numb and sated. For the time being.

His replete sigh followed me as I whispered off the bed and into the bath. He wasn't a lover now. He was a smugly satisfied man, basking in the self-adulation of conquest. I closed the bathroom door before switching on the light and running noisy water in the basin. I had to reach high for the waiting pistol. Unfolding the towel from its bluesteel deadliness, I held it loosely in my right hand, swung it up behind my back.

Johnny had been in a hell of a hurry, almost as anxious as I was. He hadn't waited to get all his clothes off. Or had he just been careful? His shoulder holster was still in place, within easy reach. Maybe Johnny was even now regretting the impulse that had brought him to a strange room with a strange woman, minus bodyguards.

Thinking, I cut off the basin faucet and started the shower. Malloy had one taste, but it had been too swift and passing. He would want more, a fuller, more flavorful enjoyment. The shower splashed. I took off my rumpled skirt and blouse and hung them over the towel rack. With the soft fluffiness of a bath towel around my hips and across my breasts like an intriguing sarong, Johnny's eyes wouldn't be on the hand he couldn't see. I shut off the water and opened the door just wide enough to slip through. The crack of light fell whitely across the bed.

I angled out of it as I went toward him. "Johnny," I said in a small voice, "you must think I'm—"

"Wonderful," he said. "And I've been getting comfortable. Hope you don't mind. This time, it's going to be even better, even more wonderful."

The shaft of light showed me his bare chest, the anticipating grin he wore. Poor Johnny, he wasn't so careful after all. His coat—and the shoulder holster—was on the chair on the other side of the bed.

"Dream on," I said softly.

"What—what did you say?"

"Keep dreaming," I repeated, the pistol swinging from behind my back. "Because there'll never be a next time for you, Johnny."

He lifted a hand to shade the bathroom light from his eyes. "I don't understand—"

"No," I said, "you don't."

And squeezed the trigger. The silencer held the explosion to a chuff! A hole appeared under his left nipple. The tang of cordite drifted around me as I leaned over Johnny Malloy and watched the permanent horror etch itself on his face. I don't think he even twitched. The slug had been dead center, tering through his heart. The Combine could scratch Malloy off its list.

Dressing quickly, I wiped everything in the room carefully, then packed the rest of my clothes and went to the window to drop the suitcase into the dark alley below. There wasn't much noise when it landed. With my handkerchief, I eased Johnny's gun out of the shoulder holster and cramped his lifeless fingers around its butt. That would give the cops something to think about.

I was calm as I went down the back stairs and out of the delivery entrance to collect my suitcase. Now maybe the Combine would believe me; now perhaps Bailey would realize he had a good businesswoman in me. What had he called me—a Black Widow?

He should have known the Widow's bite doesn't need three days to take effect. Her poison is immediate—and fatal.

CHAPTER ELEVEN

Did you ever wonder how it feels to kill a man? Of course you have. At one time or another, everybody in the world has wanted to kill somebody. Usually the idea is only momentary, passing quickly as the flash of anger wears away. Sometimes the idea sticks. That's why there are such things as gas chambers and electric chairs and the hangman's rope.

And damned fools for them to be used on. Sure, I can understand a burst of rage that blinds you to everything but the need to destroy. I understand, but I don't go along with it. Blind vengeance is for amateurs, and the amateurs get hung, or gassed or fried. The authorities get damned few professionals on death row.

Professional heisters, yes—and blackmailers, stickup artists, con men; each somehow forced into unplanned killing to protect himself. Not the coldly efficient gun for hire. Not the hit and runners. We come in, do a job, and get out. No connections, no entanglements, no real emotion.

Generally, that is. With me, it's a little different. I enjoy my work. I like the thrill of the chase, being able to lure and outsmart the guy set for the hit. And when I've got him where I want him, after I've possessed him, there's the supreme emotion. It comes when I look down the bluesteel bore of a gun and feel my finger ready on the trigger, when I see the stark terror dawning in his eyes.

It's difficult to describe how I feel then. I feel tall, huge, all-powerful. I hold death in my hand. It's up to me, Lee Carson, whether the cringing male in my sights lives or dies. I'm all the violated women on earth, all the suffering, second-rate girls everywhere. I'm the tortured, the hurt, the silently suffering, the bartered. My name is death, and my finger tightens. I kiss my lover with searing flame, with a swift spear of fatal lightning, so that he will never love another woman.

They're always so damned surprised, staring at me in horrified disbelief as I stroke the trigger. They're amazed, stunned that a tiny woman can destroy them. Especially a woman with the sweat of their lovemaking still on her body. The surprise is still branded on their faces as I punch their tickets to hell.

A split second later, I have no emotions at all. The power is gone, the feeling of mastery vanishes. I'm cold again, thinking, doing the things I have to do so I can't be traced, not getting careless, not making the one mistake that might trip me up. But once away from the scene, once free and clear, my thighs ache with need, my breasts lift themselves erect. I don't know why; I do know that the urge to be loved is almost overpowering.

Loved? What the hell is that? Love is only a four-letter work. I know others that are much more graphic, and much closer to the truth. But it's a usable word, one that the self-made censors can't strike out, because that's what makes the world go around. It says here. I know better.

Anyhow, there have been some startled guys who have "loved" me, right after I made a hit, guys who had no idea that a well-stacked girl was going to fall into their laps with no effort on their part. But of course they chalked it up to their irresistible maleness, preened their swollen egos with the thought that after all, it was only their just dues as handsome and virile men.

Men? Kids, slobs, near-animals—just so long as they were male and could give me what I needed at the moment. A gas station attendant, big-eyes and half-afraid as I practically dragged him back of the grease rack; a big-bellied fry cook, smirking through the odor of grease as he spread me quivering on a filty bed behind the cheap diner; a parking-lot kid who kept one eye on the lighted office shack as I writhed desperately beneath him on the seat of my own car.

But they served my purpose. My purpose, not theirs, no matter what they told themselves later, no matter how much they bragged to their unbelieving friends about the cute little chick who begged them to come with her. Naturally, I never went back to any of them. My need had been sharp, but transient. They lied to themselves that they had used me. It was the other way around; I had used them. And discarded them afterwards, like soiled and rumpled tissues. Why not? New and cleaner ones were cheap and plentiful. Cheap, hell—they came free.

Maybe I'd better stick closer to my story, and stop wandering off the track so much. But if I don't stray a little, this might read like a railroad time table. Still, for the sake of continuity, I'll go back to the success of my first real hit—back to Johnny Malloy. Or rather, to the events that followed.

Right after I pointed the .38 at ambitious Johnny Malloy, he became just another statistic, another series of letters chipped on a tombstone. And a bundle of cash. I could use the payoff now due from Bailey. The money from Mel Tani's deposit box needed replenishing. I had used a big chunk of it to get my name wiped off the records, spreading heavy payments around where they would do the most good.

Do you think it's impossible for somebody to stand trial, spend two years in prison, and have the records erased as if they never been? You're wrong. An underpaid clerk in the musty caverns of a newspaper morgue will lose certain file copies if the price is right. A court recorder will destroy tapes, a shrewd female convict will smuggle stolen record jackets out of prison, a safe-cracker will open a parole officer's box—if the prices are right. My prices were. Making my name disappear cost me almost thirty thousand dollars.

Sure, it would have been cheaper to change my name. But nobody changes fingerprints; nobody changes the shape of their heads and their general physical appearance. And sure, there were people around who would remember Lee Carson: cops, a judge, matrons, other cons. But they'd play hell proving anything, if the files covering Lee Carson's prints, photos, and history had vanished.

Anyway, I greased the proper palms and bought back my record. As far as the police could prove, I was clean, without arrests. I intended to keep things that way. I used almost all the. rest of the money I inherited from Mel Tani to set up a front for myself. To live in Palm Springs costs plenty, and to live the way I wanted, was even more expensive. But it would put me beyond suspicion. What cop would get nosey about a brainless, monied playgirl who spent all her time at swimming pool cocktail parties? With legitimate society friends, that is. I made certain to steer clear of involvement with any of the sharp operators.

I passed this along to Bailey through an information drop. He sent along my pay for the Malloy hit after I was established in the social whirl of Palm Springs. There was a note enclosed in the envelope with the money. It read: "Smart."

Nothing more; but I knew I was in. I knew the Combine had me high on their list as a good, trustworthy gun. With a clean hit on Johnny Malloy, I'd proven myself. From then on, I'd have plenty of jobs, because there's always some half-intelligent jerk somewhere who gets big ideas about moving in on territories that don't belong to him; always some half-cunning wheel who gets ambitions to be an even bigger wheel.

And if not, there are the minor irritants to the Combine's operations—stoolies, punks ready to trade what little they know in order to buy a few days of freedom from prison. And that's all they buy, a few days. The word goes out, and someone like me is sent in to show them what a bad bargain they made.

Naturally, the payment varies. For some punk, it's only a couple of thousand, plus expenses. For a big name, the payoff can run as high as twenty-five, thirty thousand dollars—depending upon how well he's protected and how much trouble it takes getting to him.

Anybody can be hit. If not from in close, then from a distance. Every guy has to go out sometime, and it only takes a moment to get the sights on him. Since the Army developed the sniperscope and the snooperscope, those tricky infra-red devices make it a cinch to nail a target in the black of a moonless night. All it takes is know-how and patience, and a good eye.

I'm getting ahead of myself again. I was going to tell about setting up Lee Carson as a playgirl. That part was fun. I leased a big house and hired servants. For a week or two, I'd damned near laugh aloud whenever one of the maids came near me. It was ludicrous, the girl from the hard-dirt country, the ex-con, the stripper, being catered to by servants. But I got used to them. I learned to act as if they weren't even there. That's the attitude they understand, because butlers and maids and cooks are bigger snobs than the people they work for.

I had closets bulging with expensive clothes, the white T-Bird nestling in the garage, a liquor cabinet stocked with the best, a game room and the pool. With all that glitter, it was ridiculously simple for me to establish myself as a rich girl on the loose, a thrill-seeker without family ties, but with those all-important stock dividends rolling in. In the beginning, I used to wonder what my new-found friends would say if they knew my actual stock consisted of an arsenal of carefully-hidden weapons.

But it didn't matter, because they would never know. To them, I was that deliciously loose-moraled Lee Carson, heiress to something-or-other in Virginia. The Virginia part explained the slight accent I could never manage to completely shed, and I shrugged off any slight probings of my background with jokes about hunt breakfasts and how boring the Shenandoah Valley could be. It's a damned good thing most of the desert bums knew even less about the Old South than I did. Most of them were Westerners, newly-rich oil and Hollywood people who were too busy in a constant frenzy of fun-hunting to worry about a strange girl's past. If you were good-looking and had money, you were in.

I met Wally Metcalf two nights after I came to town. He was big in a soft, indolent way, drove a Mercedes and wanted to know if I'd sleep with him.

In the contrived dimness of the cocktail lounge, I lifted an eyebrow at him. He had been on the stool beside me for exactly ten minutes before making his verbal pass.

"Sleep with you?" I asked. "Probably, mister. You look as if you might be entertaining. But not now; not just like that. If you're in a hurry, I'm sure you can find a call-girl."

I turned my back to him.

Timidly, his voice came over my shoulder. "But I thought—"

Looking into my glass, I said, "I suppose that's a compliment in some weird manner."

Wally swallowed audibly. "Ah—my apologies, Miss—"

I told him my name.

"Lee Carson," he repeated. "If I can start over, Lee Carson, I'd really like to know you better."

Wally Metcalf would know me better. He'd be damned sorry he did.

CHAPTER TWELVE

Wally was interesting. The outward aspect of him, the shambling, good-natured, little boy quality was real enough, but only one facet of a devious personality that had enough twists and turns for a dozen men. Wally Metcalf was a hedonist. The term means various things to different people. As a doctrine of Greek philosophers, hedonism was a goal, since pleasure, of whatever kind, was the only good.

Ethically, it stands for perverted physical indulgence. To psychologists, it means a tendency to exaggerate and dwell upon pleasurable sensations. But any way you cut it, it's a juicy piece of cake. Or an alibi designed to salve a nagging conscience. And it takes money to practice.

Wally had plenty of practice. I had a hint of his experience when I let him take me home that first night, but it takes more than a single impassioned blending for a woman to really know a man. The very newness of the affair tends to abruptness; the strange feel and flavor of a man's body can hurry things, and no woman likes to be hurried.

I'd let him know I wasn't a call girl, and the quiet richness of my new house proved it. Not that there's much difference between in business and one simply on the prowl, except in a man's mind. A cash payment generally takes all the zing out of his romance. Yet the same man will cheerfully pay all his mistress's bills, let her have a charge account, and buy her expensive presents. Personally, I could never see the difference.

But it meant something to Wally, although he often ordered women by the dozen and happily paid for them. This, I was to find out later, when he brought me into the pseudo-secret inner circles of Palm Springs society. For the moment, though, it was only Wally and myself in the big, white-carpeted living room, looking at each other with a tremble of eager anticipation. Open to the softness of the desert night, the glass patio doors let in an aura of flower scent, spiced and heady. Breathing deeply, I slid the light fur wrap from around my shoulders.

"The bar's over there," I said.

His eyes were all over me, probing at the mysteries barely concealed by my evening gown, licking hotly over the swells of my breasts and the moulded flaring of my thighs.

"I don't need a drink," Wally said.

"I don't, either," I murmured, and turned my back to him. "Here—I can use a little help, though. I can never understand why they put these zippers in the back."

I felt his hands twitch as he fumbled with the zipper, felt his breath warm upon my skin. Wally's lips brushed the nape of my neck, tingled at my ear. Stepping out of the gown, I swung sinuously to face him.

"T—the servants—"

"Live out," I breathed. "Wouldn't have it any other way."

And then there wasn't time for talking. My filmy bra and lace panties disappeared. The nap of the carpet was caressing my back. I said Wally was experienced; at the moment, I didn't realize just how much. It was enough to know the thrill of his body, the knowing search of his hands and mouth upon me.

I responded in a mounting frenzy, in a swiftening whirlpool of flesh and fire that spun us madly together upon the white rug, that flailed and hammered our bodies in a bubbling fury of sweet warm violence.

It was over too soon. Too quickly, the tautness flowed out of my flesh, and the slide from the pinnacle of delight was implacable. I sighed away from Wally, retreated from the grip of his hands and lifted myself to stand momentarily spent and a shade disappointed above his supine body.

He surprised me. There were fingers clamped around my ankle. Wally Metcalf wasn't finished with me. For an angry second, I fought him, innately furious at his mastery. But the battle dissolved into a strange and contorted acceptance that was more animal than human, that was the female animal being savagely ravished by her mate.

Much later, in the aseptic walls of my shower, I discovered claw marks on me. Wally put all of himself into his act. It had been a new experience, offbeat and weird. But my acceptance had been an act, too. I couldn't allow any male to dominate me for long. In any situation, Lee Carson had to be the boss. Especially where sex was concerned. What the hell made men think they were born to be the masters? What made them decide only they could take, and buy, and trade, and discard?

My new and intriguing lover would soon find that his vaunted male supremacy was a fallacy, that this woman, at least, was more than equipped to handle him. I didn't particularly care whether he liked it or not. Palm Springs was full of men.

But Wally had a stock of other surprises for me. He did like to be mastered, in turn. There was nothing this strong and pampered man didn't know about sex; there was nothing so bizarre that he hadn't tried it, at least once. In fact, Lee Carson was only a babe in the woods, in spite of her willingness to experiment. Wally was going to teach me a lot of things in the weeks to come.

From here on, some of the stories I'm going to tell may shock some people, and may sicken others. But some will find themselves nodding and saying: that's what I thought happened in those plush resorts. Still others will shake their heads and tch-tch, while underneath, they're secretly envious—because they've always wanted to do the same things. But they never had the time, the money, the opportunity—or the guts. Well, I did.

A few miles beyond the city limits, there's an isolated mansion with high-walled gardens, a huge swimming pool, a ballroom and countless bedrooms, and well-paid guards who patrol its outer perimeter with vicious dogs. Mansion, did I say? Castle might be a better word.

It's a gathering place for the sexually bored, the sensation-sated rich and the interesting and willing not-so-rich. Security regulations are tighter than those at an H-bomb plant. Entry is by special written invitation only, and those engraved cards have a hidden code mark that shows up under the gateman's fluorescent light. Would-be gate crashers and newsmen get a heave-ho so painfully professional that they never try to come back.

You might recognize the name of the owner—if you read stock market reports regularly, or if you happen to be involved in foreign oil, or if you deal in fleets of tankers. Otherwise, his name wouldn't mean much to you, and you'd probably just shrug. You'd be shrugging off one of the richest men in the world, and certainly among the top two or three most powerful. This man frowns, and kindoms sway; he snarls and countries go bankrupt.

And Saul Geli—as I'll call him—has powerful friends everywhere. Usually, they're also strange. At least, the ones I met were. There were sloe-eyed potentates from the Near East, royal expatriates from a dozen nations, playboys and playgirls from everywhere. The faces changed day by day, but the theme was the same—do as you please, to whomever you please. Almost. Geli ruled, and if his idea differed from yours, you changed your mind.

Some of the guests were the glamour girls and boys of nearby Hollywood, movie personalities whose traits and backgrounds had been carefully constructed by press agents. At Geli's place, they let themselves go, literally wallowing in the fleshpots they only symbolized on the screen.

And there were paid specialists, luscious women utterly amoral, cute men who'd perform at a suggestion.

The Roman orgies couldn't have held the proverbial candle to one of Saul Geli's parties. Oh, maybe in the torture and murder aspects, but that wasn't needed at the mansion. There were thrills enough without going that far.

Let's see if I can picture the place for you, as it was the first night I saw it. Wally Metcalf was one of Geli's favorites, and he'd wangled an invitation for me. Cautiously, he had explained that everything happened at Geli's, that we'd probably be separated from each other in the hectic uproar. I was willing.

Still, the initial scene was a jolt, even though I'd been warned what to expect. I remember standing there with one hand on Wally's arm, my mouth open and my eyes wide. We'd come through a garden entrance to the sprawling patio by the pool, and the sights there were numbing.

From where we stood, I could see thirty or forty people. Most of them were nude, and most of them were beautiful. Some of them were ugly—a few fat old men with distended bellies, a few bloated hags. It was a recreated scene from a festival of Caesar's time, the reincarnation of a Baccahalia.

Softly colored lights shifted at random across the terraces, staining the waters of the pool, stroking purples and scarlets and golds over glistening naked bodies. The fat old men were surrounded by young, slim girls; the wrinkled old women were catered to by laughing boys. There were mirrors everywhere, so that the originals were multiplied and reflected a hundred times, from a hundred angles.

Perfumed flesh and burning eyes; flowing hair and velvet skins. The cloying smell of marijuana; the aroma of fine wines and rich whiskeys. Music throbbing and sensuously primitive. A tantalizing panorama of sexuality calculated to lure the senses.

Wally drew me aside to let a pair of nude and dripping girls chase each other shrieking into the outer darknesses. We skirted a grassy, brush-hung plot where three girls and a man were tangled in twisting, impossible contortions. Wally pressed a drink into my hand, leaned to whisper in my ear.

"These are just the hangers-on, the window dressing," he said. "The real party is going on upstairs—anything you can imagine. A movie room, with couches instead of seats, and continuous shows; opium pipe entertainment in another; girls and girls, boys and boys, and spectacular combinations of each. And the big windup. That usually happens about this time."

I swallowed hard. Nothing in the simple experiences of my past had prepared me for anything like this. "T—the windup? What's that?"

Wally ran a hand over my back. "IT's kind of special. No call girls there, no hired swishes. Interested?"

"I—I might be."

He told me about it, quickly, urging me toward a room off the upper corridor. When he left me at its door and hurried on, I had a moment of panic, of indecision. Then I thought what the hell. I was here for fun, wasn't I? I turned the knob and stepped in.

A girl drifted toward me, bare except for a clinging, diaphanous material that snugged her full hips. She murmured something, and I stood still as she took off my clothes and oiled my body with a musky scent. She lifted a black hood over my head, and made certain that my hair was all tucked inside. The lazy hood covered my entire head, its drawstring drawn gently about my throat. I flinched as the girl touched my breasts, and stared down through the mask's eye-slits to find she had rouged my nipples.

When she led me to a curtained doorway, I hesitated again. Wally had said there was no hired entertainers out there, that each man had brought someone of his own, someone special. It was a hell of an idea.

I went through the curtains and joined a circle of ten other women, glancing curiously at their naked bodies, at the black hoods like my own. From what Wally had told me, these women were all dear to the men who had brought them here. Some of them were like myself, just girl friends. Others were wives, and still others far more closely related to their escorts than that.

The lights were dim, but up close, I could see they were fair and dark, tall and small, full-bodied and slim, all attractive, all different. Yet somehow, we were all strangely alike in our hoods and the vague light.

Eleven men stood across the big room, as nude as we were. They were clustered around a bar, smoking and drinking. A gong sounded, echoing through the room. The men turned from the bar. One moved toward us. I found myself in the center of a line, my hips brushing other feminine hips on each side of me. We waited.

The man wasn't young, but his body was hard and lean. Deepset eyes glittered in a tanned hawk's face. His lips were thin. He licked them as he stopped in front of the first girl and put his hands on her body. There were no sounds except the occasional husky rasps of breathing. Nobody spoke.

He ran his hands over the girl, starting at her breasts, moving slowly, searchingly down. I saw her shudder at his intimate touches. He moved to the next woman and repeated the process;

and to the next, and finally to me. His fingers were strong, yet gentle and deftly probing.

"This one," he said then, and took me by the hand to lead me from the line.

A sigh rippled through the waiting women, and another man stepped forward. My escort took me to the bar and handed me a cold glass. I gulped the liquor, unable to tear my eyes away from the scene of men choosing their partners so calmly, without fully knowing which face was beneath the impenetrable hoods that masked us all.

In the dimness, stimulated by liquor and trembling with excitement, a man might very well pick his own wife, or another girl bound to him by genetic lines. Or he might choose the wife or sister or mistress of his best friend. The not-knowing added a heady spice to the affair, an element of chance that was a thrill in itself. As I said, it was a hell of an idea.

When we were all paired off, I finished another drink and eyed the woman Wally Metcalf had chosen. She was just about my size, small and firmly put together. I wondered if he had been searching for me, or if I'd been included in this gathering because the girl and I were physically alike.

Brushed first by this naked body, then by that one, I was tense, on edge, ready to go with the man who had picked me from the line. But no couple seemed ready to move out of the room. In a few minutes, I knew why.

This was the room. No waiting bed in seclusion, no private couch down the hallway; only this. Only the thickly carpeted floor; only the fat silken pillows scattered about. The first couple drifted into a corner, and sank down together. Then another pair, beside and almost touching a man and woman next to them.

I took a deep breath. I couldn't say I hadn't been warned. There were gently insistent hands upon my own hips, and I was thankful for the mask that hid my face. Why not, I thought rag-gedly, as I lowered myself to become another rhythmically mov-ing cog in the erotic machinery—why the hell not?

Peering through the slits in my hood, my eyes roamed the room, never closing, fascinated by the sights around me. The hawk-faced man was strong and tender, and in no hurry. That suited me fine, and I adjusted myself to mesh with him, to blend my tremulous body to his own.

It was only a minute before all that changed. The compulsion within me boiled out, sweeping everything before it, drowning the maleness of my temporary lover in the thrusting, greedy rage of my feminine power. I fought the man, there on the floor of the room, fought him and conquered him, taking instead of giving, raping instead of being raped.

Almost an hour later, when the couples had eddied away from their communal bridal chamber into more private sur-roundings, I found that the man who had chosen me was Saul Geli himself. And I also found that he wouldn't make that mistake again. Geli was too used to being master; with me, he couldn't be. I didn't bother to tell him that no man could.

Dawn was breaking when a tired and surfeited Wally Metcalf drove us out through the big, guarded gates of the Geli estate. He would have made a day of it, if I hadn't insisted he take me home. Anything taken in too-large doses is liable to sicken—and that goes for sex, too.

Don't get me wrong. Lee Carson is a hell of a long way from even the suggestion of prudery, and I won't claim the night hadn't excited me almost beyond belief, or that I wouldn't go back for more of the same. It was just that, at the moment, I was groggy, tired, needing sleep and time to absorb all I had seen and done.

And maybe I had a hunch. After all, the rest of those people didn't have to work for a living. I did, and my hunch centered around that fact.

I was right. After Wally dropped me off at my home, a quiet and nondescript man was waiting on my patio. Wordlessly, he handed me an envelope. It was the contract for another hit.

CHAPTER THIRTEEN

A s usual, Bailey's bird-dogs were thorough. All the information needed was included inthe envelope with a substantial expense advance. The money would be needed, since my target was in Miami, and I had to go there the long way around.

I left a note for Wally Metcalf, packed one large suitcase, and taxied to the airport for the early jet East. Because of my cover act of being from an old Virginia family, I bought a round trip ticket to Richmond. It would be a bother, flying out of there under a different name to Atlanta, where I'd pick up a car for the rest of the trip. It would also be a hell of a lot safer. If I learned anything during my jolt in prison, it was to cover my tracks, to think at least one step ahead of the law.

If, by some wild off-chance, some cop at this end got suspicious, Miss Lee Carson left town on business, flew back home to Richmond. The story would check out. I'd even register at a hotel there and mess up the bed before going back to the airport. Nobody would trail me to Atlanta, and nobody would possibly connect me with a hit in Miami. All clear, all thought out. When I stopped thinking things out, I'd be as good as dead.

On the plane, I avoided all contacts and camouflaged Bailey's typewritten info sheet in a magazine, memorizing every detail. The guy's name was Frankie Fry, a small-time bookie who'd gotten ideas about moving into the alky business. Frankie should have stayed with his two dollar bets.

The description was complete, matching the picture of the man. He looked small-time. Frankie was a dapper, a bandbox character with a pencil-line moustache and a yen for young, small girls. That was a break. The little guys generally go after big, hefty women, trying to make up for their lack of stature that way. Did you ever notice the type of girls jockeys marry? All tall, bosomy strippers.

But back to Frankie, who liked them young, inexperienced and unprofessional. School kids were his choice, college freshmen on vacation, tender girls out of the Florida swamps. Okay, I'd play it his way. There were no lines in my face yet, and in the right clothes, I'd look about eight years younger. A bobby-soxer relaxing on the beach, catching up on her homework; cute, studious and naive. Only one of my big books would contain more than the writer intended. A fat sociology textbook was a natural for hiding a gun. The center of the pages cut out, a .38 snuggled into the shell, covers closed, and I was in business. All I had to do was wait for the right time. After I allowed Frankie Fry to pick me up, of course.

Was I taking a chance, merely planting myself in Frankie's usual prowling area and hoping to be noticed? Not really. A girl can always call attention to herself by little things—a "careless" sprawling of legs, so that a short skirt exposes an inch or two of thigh; a deep, sweater-filling breath at the proper moment; a wide-eyed look of attraction. Men aren't half as smart as they think they are.

Besides, if Frankie didn't see me the first day or so, he would sooner or later. I had plenty of time. The clock was only running out for Frankie. And if he picked another girl to stay wrapped up with for a week or so, I could always stake out and pop him from a distance.

Naturally, that wouldn't be as satisfying to me. I liked to stare into a man's eyes when he realized he was going to die. And somehow, it seemed far better if I made the hit immediately after he'd made love to me, after he'd played the mighty conqueror. Standing over them, gun in my hand, completely naked, I liked to watch the conqueror dissolve, to see the gutless rabbit take its place.

But if I couldn't set Frankie up the way I wanted, I was prepared for the other way. Broken down into its component parts in my suitcase, wrapped in frilly underthings, was an M-2 carbine with a 30-round banana clip and an infra-red night-sighting device. That weapon had come a devious course from some Army supply room, getting more expensive with each pair of hands it passed through. But it was worth the price. Light, not too loud, able to pick off a man in total blackness, the carbine was a beauty. There was only one drawback. Silencers don't work a damn on any gun that operates on a recoil kickback. Still, people seldom notice the quick, flat pop of a small rifle. Even if they do, they rarely bother to report it; they're too afraid of making damned fools of themselves.

So, either way I played it, Frankie Fry was already a dead man, in all reality only marking time until I picked the place and the time. Maybe that was part of the attraction my targets have always held for me. In some strangely warped way, it's like making love to a corpse. I always know for sure that I'm the last woman they'll ever love, and I guess I get a kick out of giving them a good send-off.

I went through each of my trail-covering motions without incident, and picked up the three-year-old dark car the Combine had waiting for me on the outskirts of Atlanta. It's a long drive from there to Miama, and most of the country isn't much to see. Before I'd driven halfway, I found myself becoming oddly moody, and decided that being back in the deep South was the cause. Remember, I'd been away from home—or what passed for home in Mississippi for several years, and a lot had happened in that time. I had been living in an entirely different world.

Coming back was like re-entering a prison. The climate was muggy and insect-ridden, the very atmosphere sullen and suspicious. Even though the terrain, with its flat palmetto fields, water oaks and strangler figs, was much different than Mississippi's red clay and piney woods, it was still the South. It was oppressive, sweaty, narrow, stupid. And being there upset me, brought back too damned many memories.

I was glad to get into Miami, because the coarse glitter and neon come-on was where I belonged now. The scrawny, skittish girl I had been was dead. She died for keeps when she was spread-eagled on her mother's bed by a pair of moonshine-soaked rapists. Let her lie in peace.

Lee Carson was here now, tooling the car into a medium-priced motel, feeling the hurry-hurry of Miami's nearby Strip wash over me, a cynical and sophisticated part of the sucker-baiting, the money-spenders. I checked in under a name as phony as the license plates on my car, smiled off an unctuous offer by the desk man to help me with my bag, and took a long, cold shower.

Frankie Fry was was an afternoon operator, since he could find more young kids on the beach then, so there was no hurry. I walked to a corner store and bought notebooks and cigarettes. A block away, I got a fifth of bourbon and went back to the air-conditioned comfort of my room. I'd forgotten just how miserably hot it can be down South.

The liquor didn't help a hell of a lot. When I finally went to sleep, I still had vaguely terrifying dreams where I ran and ran from some hulking and formless horror, and woke up trembling.

Morning was welcome. I went out into it and found a book store where I picked up thick books on Sociology, Psychology and Antropology II. Even someone as unhappy as I could see that the "liberals" of the day were even more mixed-up about things. The books were meant to be answers to the problems of our day, but all they tried to prove was that there were no answers. A quick trip through a teen shop completed my equipment—white shorts and halter, a schoolgirl skirt and socks, a couple of sheer blouses, and clips to put my hair into a ponytail. When I made myself a little giggly, a bit flattered and sort of afraid, the picture would be complete. Frankie Fry would have his young kid. He'd sure as hell never be around to watch her grow up.

CHAPTER FOURTEEN

I felt his shadow fall across me before I saw it through the tint of my sun glasses. I saw the dressy white bucks in the polished sand of the beach, but pretended to continue reading my Antropology book. My towel was folded beside me, held down by two other books and folders. The too-heavy Sociology text was on the bottom, the snub-nosed Cobra .38 hidden inside it. Who knew—maybe I could make the hit and be out of the state by night. The quicker, the better.

The voice was too young. "Tough subject, and kinda' dry."

I looked up. "I don't think you're old enough to buy me a beer."

He frowned down at me. "Look—I didn't mean—"

"I know what you meant, junior," I said. "But I'm busy, okay?"

Reddening, he scuffed in the sand and muttered, "Okay, if that's how you want it."

I didn't bother to answer. I could pick up an eager kid any day, but it was good to know he'd mistaken me for one of his own kind. But he was right, in one way. Anthropology II was dry reading. All that jazz about the dawn of man. You'd think the males did the whole thing by themselves.

The next voice came from over my shoulder. It was oily smooth: "Heard what you told the kid. If you really want a beer, I'm old enough to buy it."

Closing the book, I glanced up. "I–I don't know. I was just being flip, I guess. I don't really like beer."

Under his moustache, his teeth were even and white. "I don't either. Down for the weekend?"

I took off my sun glasses. "From Roanoke U—that's up in Virginia. Thought I'd cram for a makeup exam and get a little sun at the same time."

His smile broadened. "Folks with you?"

I looked away, shifted the book on my lap. "I don't think—"

"It's any of my business? True, but I'll bet you're here alone, or with a girl friend. That's my business—betting the odds."

This was my boy, all right. He'd tossed in that last bit of information for its glamour effect upon a naive kid, conjuring up visions of the mysterious and intriguing gambler, the man-of-the-world. I damned near laughed in his face.

Instead, I showed exactly what he expected, a tentative, shy interest. He spread a big handkerchief on the sand and moved in beside me. I let him talk, conscious of his quick glances at my legs. Frankie was smooth, all right, moving deftly from subject to subject, always adding to the aura of adventure calculated to appeal to a young girl.

And I responded in kind, obviously thrilled at the attentions of an older man, fluttery and a bit frightened, but drawn to him in spite of myself. Frankie Fry ate it up. He even told me his right name. Yes, I said, hesitantly, I supposed it would be all right if he bought me just one drink; but he might get in trouble. If somebody asked for my driver's license—

"Don't worry about that," Frankie said. "I know my way around, and a lot of people are anxious to do favors for me. Now there's this quiet little place just outside of town that really swings. I'll guarantee that nobody will ask how old you are."

"Well—"

But of course I went with him. I even let him carry my books to his ornate convertible parked off the beach. I wasn't worried about the loaded sociology book falling open; it was fixed with some near-invisible strips of cellophane tape. Besides, Frankie was being gentlemanly and solicitous, and handled my things as if they were preciously fragile.

I noticed a man follow us from the beach. He was bulky, with sunburn peeling from a square face. And walked as if his legs were tired. In the parking lot, I saw him again. There were car keys in his hand, and he shuffled away. But when I looked back as the convertible roared off, he was staring after Frankie's car.

I could see how Frankie was successful with young college girls. Suave, courteous, his approach was insidiously perfect. He held open doors, lighted my cigarette, drew out my chair from the table. Kids aren't quite used to such treatment.

And I was supposed to be dazzled by Frankie's casual mention of large sums of money, by his open-handed largess to doormen and waiters. We left my books in his car. In the club, I asked him to order something for me—anything that wasn't too strong. I wasn't used to anything potent, I told him.

If I hadn't know better, the Singapore Slings would have seemed innocuous enough—tall, frosted glasses, all pretty and pink and sugary. And loaded with enough powerful gin to satisfy a seasoned boozer. I let Frankie urge a second one upon me, and deliberately turned gay and silly. His eyes gleamed, and occasionally his tongue darted swiftly out to touch his lips. Everything was going according to plan, Frankie thought.

I spilled about half of the third Sling, and giggled inanely until Frankie said it was time he took me home. I made some inept crack about not giving a damn where home was, and leaned heavily against him as he guided me back to the car.

It looked neat for my boy. In the club, I'd rattled on about how I didn't care at all for boys my own age, about how glad I was to be away from the family, and even threw in some insipid details about the strict discipline at good old Roanoke U. Did Frankie think girls my age should have to be in bed by eleven o'clock? No, Frankie didn't. He thought I was old enough to know my own mind, and most fun didn't get started until after midnight, did it?

I went "oooh," in the car, but insisted with closed eyes that I wouldn't be sick. Not that Frankie gave a damn. Leaning back in the seat, my ponytail bobbing in the wind, I sneaked looks at him through shuttered lashes, and saw the pleased smirk on his mouth. I allowed my knees to spread themselves, let the vagrant breeze slide my skirt high on my thighs. Head wobbling loosely, I wondered silently whether he'd try to talk me into going to his place, or just lead me stumbling inside.

He sort of combined the moves, murmuring in my ear as he steered me into a darkened motel cottage obviously kept for just such pickups. Nothing to worry about, he whispered. I could sleep it off here. He wouldn't bother me. The hell he wouldn't.

I balked at the door, hanging back, tugging at his arm. "B— books," I muttered. "Gotta' have my books. Mustn't—mustn't lose 'em."

He was eager. "Later, baby. They'll be okay in the car."

Swaying, I peered at him. "Gotta' have my books. Got an Anthro—anthropology exam next week. Please—"

"Okay, okay. Don't sit down here, baby. You can rest inside."

I leaned against the door until he came back with the books. Inside, the place was rigged like a bachelor's dream—hi-fi, a portable bar, nudes on the walls, but no couch and no chairs. Only the kingsize bed, beckonging with crimson satin sheets. Even the drapes were sexy, dark red and shielding the windows. The color of blood, I thought.

Frankie placed the books on the floor beside the bed. "Another drink?"

Plopping onto the scarlet sheets, I shook my head. "I—I couldn't. Just wanna' sleep."

"Sure," he said, "sure, baby—just lie back and relax. Everything will be okay."

Yeah. Okay for Frankie Fry. Only moments after my head touched the covers, I felt him sliding the lowheel shoes from my feet, felt him peel away my bobby sox. Then he waited, listening to my deep breathing. His hands were sly on my ankles, sliding gently up over both calves, pausing at my knees. I didn't stir, although excitement was beginning to build within me, the blood starting to race through my veins.

I was thinking of more than the caress of his fingers as they felt cautiously for the zipper of my skirt. I thought of the books almost in reach, of the bluemetal pistol waiting in oiled and deadly precision. But that would come in due order; now was the moment to moan softly and roll slightly upon the bed— "unconsciously" helping my cunning lover-to-be to whisk away my skirt.

Frankie was anxious, but careful. He didn't want a startled, screaming girl on his hands. Especially one who was supposed to be underage. He also wanted things readied to his complete satisfaction. That meant I was to be stripped bare, that he desired me wholly nude, to fondle and pet my supposedly very young body. I let him work away, my flesh tightening, straining toward his touch. But I didn't wriggle, didn't shed the pretense of being passed out.

Until his lips got too enthusiastic, until his eager body fitted itself to mine in a demanding rhythm. Eyes squeezed shut, I thought raggedly that my responses now could be considered as automatic, subconscious, as the motions of a girl reacting to a deft lover with the very fibers of her being. Frankie Fry was beyond noticing. His mouth was hard and seeking mine, forcing my lips open. His hands were brutally possessive, clutching, forcing me to lift, to swing my hips.

In a moment, I thought. In a moment, the bright ecstasy can be reached, caught, held, dissolved by the rippling thunder that was shaking me from head to foot. In a moment—and I struggled to bring the shining tide closer, fought to capture it when it came.

Trapped in the madwild fury, entangled in sweetwarm violence, I coiled and uncoiled, my legs tapered, golden serpents. The man with me was all man, every male, loved and hated, needed and scorned. My sobbing cry of completion broke against the even whiteness of his teeth as my frenzied fingers raked at the quivering muscles of his back.

Together, we were softquiet in the backwash of expended passion, melting, limp upon the crimson sheets that had been tangled by our feet. Slowly, I drew away from Frankie.

"You woke up in a hell of a hurry," he said in a drowsy voice.

I didn't answer until I was off the bed. Crouching at the pile of books, I thumbnailed the tape from the biggest one, flipped the cover back and took the pistol from its hollow nest.

Then I said, "Yeah—didn't I?"

Something in my tone warned him. His eyes snapped open, and he turned on his side to face me. When he saw the muzzle of the .38 gaping at him, Frankie stiffened and pawed for his discarded shorts. Staring at me, at the gun I held in a steady fist, he wadded the shorts to cover himself, seeking a hopeless kind of security by hiding his threatened manhood.

Like Johnny Malloy, I thought. Just like Johnny Malloy. And probably identical to other names and other men to come, to be pinned motionless by the nearness of death on other rumpled beds.

"What—" he gasped.

"You're on the short end of the odds this time, bookie," I said. "You should have stayed with across-the-board bets. Distilling alky is over your head."

I stood up, took a pair of careful steps back out of a sudden grab.

"T—the Combine? But—no, you wouldn't just shoot me. No. Listen, listen to me. Money—I got a lot of money. Forty grand—fifty. A cut of the business. Don't—don't—"

The cold snick of the hammer earing back was loud in the heavy air of the room.

"I have a contract," I said. "You know how it is."

Frankie's face took on a skull-like sunkenness, a parchment color. The tip of his tongue tried to dampen lips that peeled away from his teeth.

"You—you're no kid," he hissed. "You're no kid—"

And tried for the door.

He had the galvanic speed of fear, the swiftness of desperation, rolling off the bed away from me. His knees hit the floor and he sprang up and out, arms pumping frantically, eyes bulging, mouth wide.

Frankie's hand was pawing at the knob when the first bullet caught him. It smashed into the base of his spine and hammered him into the door panel. He went on tiptoe, then sagged and began to spin slowly toward me, agony etched in every line of his body.

I shot him again, spotting the heavy slug just over his right ear. The bite of powdersmoke was tangy around me, filling my flared nostrils.

I stood over him. "No," I said, "I'm no kid, Frankie. I'm very old. I'm old as death."

CHAPTER FIFTEEN

Later, I was to blame the episode on the South itself, on the depressive atmosphere, on the clinging heat and the dull-eyed people. Probably this was only rationalizing away something that never should have happened at all.

Hell, I'm a professional. I had no business letting personalities enter my life. Emotions are for other people—the tender thoughts, the mental entanglements, that is. Love and hate are sticky webs that can entrap the unwary. I didn't have to worry about the love part. That was for suckers. Simple lust can easily take its place. Frill lust up with all the wildly erotic imagining possible, and "love" seems wan and pallid.

But hate? That's a luxury I couldn't afford, either, but I was too new at this business to realize that. I had the power for revenge, why not use it?

Of course it was the Finneys, Jett and Pete. Indirectly, they'd killed my poor shadow of a mother. More to the point, they'd done their damndest to rub their filth off on me. They'd driven me from the only home I'd ever known. And they'd sent me straight into the bed of a stranger, forced me into marrying a cheap drummer who'd taken my body and sold my respect.

Returning the car I'd driven from Miami at the Combine garage outside Atlanta, I bought a one-way ticket to the Mississippi airport nearest Shuba. I was going "home." To kill two men.

On the plane, I thought of the dismantled carbine nestling in my suitcase, the infra-red sighting device. The .38 I'd used on Frankie Fry was rusting in the primeval ooze of an off-trail Florida slough, guarded by screens of cabbage palms and saw-tooth palmetto, shrouded with thick greenscum water and sen-tried by cottonmouth moccasins and alligators. Nobody would ever find that gun. No ballistics expert would ever match up its bore marking with the slugs in Frankie Fry's corpse. And even if it was possible to resurrect the misshapen chunk of rust the .38 would be in a couple of weeks, so what? It couldn't be traced to me.

For some reason, I suddenly remembered the chunky, bald-ing man on the beach in Miami—the man whose sunburned face had been turned after Frankie's car as we drove away from the parking lot. His image nagged at the edges of my mind. I shrugged it off. Another tourist, probably. If not that, then just some local mutely leching after a cute "schoolgirl," maybe seeing the pickup on the sand and drooling dreamfully after us.

But the hell with Florida and its denizens. The state of Mississippi was unfolding itself off the right wingtip of the plane. In a few minutes, I'd be stepping off the ramp onto my native soil. The timing was right, too.

It was late afternoon, giving me a chance to buy a ramshackle car for a couple of hundred; giving me another hour to drive South to Shuba and arrive just after sunset. By avoiding the main highway and skirting the thin cluster of buildings called town, I could circle over dirt back-country roads and come out close to the homestead. Close enough to make my way unobserved to the shack. After that, I'd have to go on instinct and incident.

I didn't doubt that the Finneys would be there. Where else would they go? They didn't have brains nor ambition enough to do anything except scratch for vegetables on the wornout land, plink rabbits and squirrels and make bad whiskey. And chase after the frightened mulatto girls down on the banks of the Chickasawhay River.

Behind the wheel of a rattling, wheezing jalopy that a salesman had been happy to get rid of, I turned off the highway onto the dirt road by the sawmill, and felt the piney woods smell and coolness close over me. It was dusk, the best part of the day in that part of the country. A bullbat angled tilting across the road, piping hungry for night-flying insects. Off in the trees, a whippoorwill sang lonely in gathering darkness.

The car grunted around a curve, dim headlights peering blindly, and I slammed on the brakes. They held—shuddering the car to a halt bare inches from the water that was pouring across a dip in the road, muddy water that purled hissing around the bridgeposts atop the crossing.

I cursed, thinking that I had been gone too long, that I should have remembered this was high-water time in Clark County, that every Spring, downpours filled the creeks and rivers and sent them out of their banks to rage along the bottomlands. The farmers here paid little attention, if the water didn't crawl right up into their houses. The inundation enriched the fields near the creeks, gave them new strength to grow cotton. And it was a time for laying in fish, for setting trot-lines and set-hooks in the sprawling waters, for wounded minnows and gutted crawfish to tempt the big mudcats washed down from the northern tributaries in their forced migration out of the Yazoo and the Tchufuncta.

I smiled. Now I knew exactly where one of the Finneys would be. The old man would be in his leaky skiff, poling from one heavily weighted fishline to another, making his bi-daily check to haul in tired catfish and rebait the hooks. Jett Finney, my stepfather in name, would be in his glory, gathering the free food, actually working harder at his annual sport that he did all the rest of the year.

I backed the car until I found a turnoff. I remembered another road, little more than a trail, that would lead me to the county road that skirted the home place. If it was open, I'd reach home in time to stalk Jett Finney from the water-filled gullies.

The trail was open, and I turned off the car's lights a half-mile from the shack, coasting downhill the last fifty yards before turning off into a familiar, brush-choked cowpath to hide it. I took the carbine from my suitcase and put it together, fitting the bulky snooperscope to its stock and slipping the 30-round clip into the breech. In slacks and lowheel shoes, I slipped along the road to the fringes of the watercovered bottomland, listening, nerves tensing up as I thought of the hundreds of water moccasins that were in the brush now, flood-driven to higher ground.

There was a faint, muffled thump of wood-on-wood, a change in the sound of the rushing creek. Jett Finney was running true to form. The sound was that of his pole against the side of the old skiff. I heard it again, closer. Jett was coming in.

Putting my right eye to the rubber cup of the scope, I thumbed the butterfly switch that kicked the enclosed battery into operation and scent a scanning beam of invisible light lancing into the darkness for twenty or thirty yards. Moving the muzzle slowly, I saw the outlines of dripping treetops, a floating log with a glistening snake stretched across it, and—the skiff, the vagueness of the pole in Jett Finney's hands, Jett himself, stopped and grunting.

My finger tightened on the trigger; the crosshairs of the sight had him centered. I could space three or four quick ones into his scrawny chest before he hit the water. But I hesitated, the cautious pattern of my business nagging at me. Jett's bloated, turtle-chewed body would hang up somewhere downriver, sooner or later. The waters would recede, and somebody would find what was left of him. A coroner might poke around in the stinking mess and discover the bullet holes. And this was one killing I might possibly be connected to.

It was only an off-chance that someone would remember the kid who'd hated her stepfather, the kid who'd run away one night without a word to anybody. But it's the off-chances that knot a rope around a neck. I took my finger off the trigger, kept my eye to the sight as Jett poled the skiff in to the bank.

He grounded the boat and threw his pole out. Then he turned, balancing precariously and stopped to fumble in the skiffs bottom for his string of catfish and the extra sinkers, lines and hookd he always carried to replace the ones driftwood might tear away. I put down the carbine and blinked rapidly to adjust my eyes to the dark without the snooper light. Bending low, I eased toward the skiff, with nothing but my hands and an idea. Water noises covered any sounds I might have made, and I felt for the pole Jett had tossed onto the bank.

Just as my fingers closed around its long wetness, I heard him grunt and step out of the boat. I came in hard and fast, the pole braced against one hip, guiding its end at the black outline of him. It crashed into his chest with a solid, startling thump, and I held tightly to it as Jett Finney staggered flailing backward and fell into the deep, murky waters.

Lets apart, the pole balanced out and down, I waited for him to try and crawl out onto the bank. Aiming at the splashing splutter of his head, I struck savagely—once, twice—and the noise stopped. There in the dark, wet woods, I listened for a long time. And heard nothing. Then I threw the pole far out into the rushing water and leaned down to get a good grip on the prow of the skiff. Digging my feet in, I shoved it out into the current, then scuffed the damp earth to blur any footprints.

Let some coroner get curious now. He wouldn't find a damned thing except a drowned man, a clumsy, boozing farmer who'd fallen out of his boat and banged his head on something. No bullet holes. Nothing to point an accusing finger at the farmer's runaway stepdaughter.

One down, one to go. I turned away fromthe creek, sorry only that Jett Finney hadn't had the time to know who killed him. I found my carbine again, picked it up and cradled it close to me. Now for Pete Finney. If I worked it right, this one would have plenty of time to know his executioner.

Working my way through the woods toward the light in the shack I'd grown up in, I felt peculiar, mixed-up. I wasn't certain why. You might think I felt regret, that I was afraid because I'd killed a man. Like hell. It wasn't that at all. I was glad I'd wiped Jett Finney off the earth, and I wasn't a damned bit afraid of any improbable consequences.

But he was the first man I'd killed without having him. Sexually, I mean. And the post-death reaction was setting in, the compulsive, irritating demand of hungry loins and erectile breasts. The sudden need for a man was a basic part of my psychological pattern, crying to be satisfied. And the nearest man happened to be Pete Finney.

Biting hard upon my lips as I eased closer to the house. I told myself that this couldn't be, that I didn't want Pete Finney at any price. My skin crawled as I imagined his dirty hands moving over me. Yet the pulsing insistence of my stimulated body hammered at me, demanding release of a constantly building pressure.

No, no. Not Pete. I couldn't accept him into the secret places of my flesh, couldn't possibly give him the warmth and clinging of my body. I shuddered, torn between equally powerful urges, between clammy loathing and raging desire.

Tensely, I lifted my head and peered through the grimed window. Yellow lamplight flickered inside, showing me Pete Finney slouching by the dead fireplace, the ever-present Mason jar of colorless stump-juice whiskey on the rickety table beside him. His bare, crusted feet were propped on a gnarled, sootblack slab of pine wood.

I hated him through the flyspeck glass, hated the knobby wrists with their curlings of pale hair, hated the slack wet mouth, the mean and beady eyes idiot-staring at nothing. I'd give him something to stare at, I thought. I'd give Pete Finney a sight to make his bloodshot eyes bug out.

It had to be good, had to be a trick that would lull his naturally suspicious backwoods mind. And yet I didn't dare get too far away from my gun. I thought it over, turning the problem to see every angle. I'd have to leave the carbine outside the door, depending for protection upon the stunts I'd learned in night clubs, the disabling attacks used by bored and efficient bouncers I'd watched. Thinking hard, I stared at the empty fireplace, at the jar of corn liquor, at Pete's vacuous face.

Propping the loaded carbine on the sagging porch, I opened the door and went quickly in without knocking.

"Pa?" Pete said without turning.

I made my voice small and husky. "No, Pete. It's me, Lee. I've—I've come home."

He jerked around, almost knocking over the jug. "Lee?"

I hung my head, took a few timid steps forward. "If—if you and your Pa will have me, I've come home."

His eyes glittered. He rubbed a dangling hand across his mouth. "Now, ain't this somethin'. Little uppity Lee, come crawling back like a whipped hound. Them big-city fellers run you off, Lee?"

"S—something like that," I murmured. "Pete—I'm very tired and hungry. Could you put in a word for me with your Pa?"

He smirked. "Pa's out running the set hooks. Anyhow, why should I help you? You never done nothin' for me—'cept bust my knee and cripple me for life."

I shifted from one foot to the other. "I'm sorry about that, Pete. I was awful young and scared. I—I've learned a lot of things since then."

His eyes ranged over me, taking in the hip-moulding slacks, the way my blouse outlined my breasts. "Yeah," he said. "I 'spect you had a lot of teachers. You look right good, Lee."

"Then—then I can stay?"

He got up from the chair. "That depends on if'n you're good as you look, depends on how you act."

I nodded, slipping past him to the table and the jar of whiskey. "I've changed, Pete. More than you think. Here—here, I'll show you." And I tilted the jar for a long, burning drink of raw liquor.

"Mighty pretty," he said. "Didn't even screw up your face. Have another and show me again."

I drank, nearly choking over the coal oil taste, and handed the jar to him. He proved his superior manhood by swallowing half the contents, but he couldn't keep his eyes from watering.

"Here," I said again, "watch me, Pete; like me."

I squirmed out of the slacks, shed the blouse and stood before him in my underthings. I didn't have to simulate the quickening of my breath, the excited lift of my breasts. Pete reached for me without preliminaries.

I took back the liquor jar. "Let me get drunk, Pete. Please, so I can show you all I learned. You'd be surprised how many tricks I know now. But I ought to be good and drunk."

He showed yellow teeth in a braying laugh. "Why, shore. I reckon I know how you feel, comin' back whipped and all. I'll bust open another jug."

That was what I wanted—the fiery, potent whiskey pouring down him, adding fuel to the fire he'd long ago started. If I could just hold him off long enough, tease him along and keep him drinking, he'd be helpless for me. I'd learned to judge Pete Finney's capacity long ago, and figured he was past the halfway point already.

I had to sit on his lap and allow his pawing hands to prod and poke; I had to let him pour his fetid breath between my lips as his stubbled mouth bruised me. I had to do a lot of things while I poured the whiskey down him, faking my own drinks and giggling when I wanted to throw up.

But at last, his head wobbled. At last, he swayed and blinked stupidly, and missed me when I got up off his lap and stood back from him. Spit flecked the corners of his mouth as he pawed helplessly in the air and muttered disjointed words.

I didn't hit him very hard, but the sooty pine knot made a satisfying thump against his head. Pete slid out of the chair onto the floor.

I won't go into detail as to what I did, then. I'm not sure I like to remember it, or that I can recall it all. The next scene is clearer to me, the one where I was standing out in the yard, watching the red flames lick at the old, rotted walls of the shack. I still had the hammer in my hand. The fire roared louder. Carefully, I wiped the hammer and flung it far into the brush.

There was time to wait, the carbine pointed toward the doorway. This was the piney woods; the nearest neighbors were seven miles off. They wouldn't hurry to the fire. Nobody in Clark County would hurry to give the Finneys a hand.

I could see Pete Finney inside the blazing shack. The bright light showed me his face, the horror and cringing indecision etched sharply there. It wasn't as if I hadn't given Pete a choice.

He could take his pick: use the dull file I'd placed in his hand to saw himself free of the nails that were driven between his legs, pinning him to the floor—or he could sit there and preserve his manhood while he burned to death.

A hell of a decision for any man to be faced with? Not being a man, I couldn't say ... I do know that Pete Finney couldn't quite decide. He'd make a motion with the file, then stop and flinch up at the roof crackling over his head.

I guess he waited too damned long to make up his mind. I never did get to see whether he made a last, desperate attempt or not, because the roof fell in.

Behind me in Mississippi, I left two dead men, a shack burned to the ground, and a jalopy coasted off a steep roadbed into a river a couple of miles outside of town. I walked the rest of the way, staying in shadows until I found a cab. At the airport I went through the usual routine of getting a ticket under a name picked from the air. But this time I was too weary to play games about my destination. Who the hell would be checking me out?

I'd made a mistake ever coming back. The best thing I could do now was shake the red dust of Mississippi from my feet. The vengeance I'd wreaked didn't affect me as I'd expected. It lay with a bitter taste in my mouth, dry and flat. I guess burned-out hate always has that flavor.

It was a damned good thing there was a contract waiting for me when I got back to Palm Springs. Otherwise, I might have flipped, eating myself out with an emotional mixmaster that I couldn't turn off. As it was, I had three wild days and nights with Wally Metcalf and his amorous friends, and I needed the amoral releases.

But there was a new ingredient waiting for me in my plush playground—a chunky, balding man who walked heavily, and whose sunburned face was still peeling.

CHAPTER SIXTEEN

I saw him while Wally and I were paying a fun call on one of Palm Spring's weird characters. Elva Beacon was short and rotund, walked pitty-pat, and shook all over when she laughed, which was often. She'd blush like a schoolgirl—after coming out with some of the damndest cracks. This alone made Elva a rarity, since she was also the madame of a stable of high-priced call girls.

The guy was across the sitting room, propped tiredly against the corner bar. I stared at him for a long moment, trying to place him, trying to line up those strangely familiar, nondescript features with some incident in the past. You know how a thing like that will nag at you—you're certain you know the man, but you can't quite place him. And you don't want to walk right up and ask.

I didn't like his looks. He had none of the vacant gaiety of the drunken John out for a good time; his mouth was too hard, his eyes too watchful. And he was trying just a little too hard to be very ordinary. This man had something in common with Combine lieutenants: a careful anonymity, a practice of not being conspicuous.

I watched him over Wally's shoulder, wondering, warned by an inherent instinct. Another gunner I'd met somewhere? I wasn't sure, but I knew I'd seen him before, and I knew I didn't want to see him again. There was a smell of trouble about the man—trouble for Lee Carson.

"Wally," I murmured, in the wake of one of Elva's ribald anecdotes, "I'm a little tired. Would you mind taking me home?"

Elva chortled hugely. "Tired? Why, when I was your age, it'd take a dozen young studs like Wally to make me draw a deep breath. You gettin' old, Lee?"

I grinned at her. "That's the idea. Wally?"

He pouted. "But I had a lot of plans for tonight."

"They'll keep," I said, and walked toward the red-curtained exit from Elva's place. I felt the balding man's eyes on my back.

In my own foyer, I stood listlessy under Wally's roving hands, unresponsive. After awhile, he grunted and stepped back. "Okay, Lee. I'll call you tomorrow."

"Sorry, Wally," I said. "It's not you," and chastely kissed him good night.

Alone in the big house with the servants gone for the evening, I poured myself a drink and carried it to the edge of the patio, where I stood sipping it and frowning out at the night. I didn't know why the hell I was worrying. There was no reason I could put a mental finger upon. All my hits had been clean and professional, with no mistakes, with no leads that could possibly point to Lee Carson.

Or had they? I ran through the long list of names, tried to recall the exact details of each job. And stopped when I thought about returning "home." The Finneys, the for-free kills urged upon me by festering memories. But nobody had seen me around Shuba. Certainly not the sunburned man.

When the doorbell buzzed, I jumped a foot and sloshed liquor over the edge of my glass. Who the hell—

He stood framed in the doorway, backgrounded by the soft desert night. "I'm Jim Wirkus," he said in a dry, toneless voice. "I persuaded Elva to give me your address."

I glared at him, at the raggedy peeling of sunbaked skin, at the faint reflection of the houselights on his thinning pate. "Elva will hear about that. Say what you came to say. Then get the hell off my porch." A faded, sandy eyebrow lifted at me. "That doesn't sound like a Virginia blueblood talking. It sounds more like a backwoods wench, or like some two-dollar hooker who's done time—say in Corona."

Something cold nestled in the pit of my stomach. I took a step back, thinking of the carqine planted behind a sliding wallboard indistinguishable from those around it, of the oiled .45 revolver wrapped in waterproof cloth and hidden in a niche outside the upper bathroom window. Backwoods, Corona prison—whoever the man was, whatever reason he had for coming to my house, he knew too damned much about me, knew things I thought had been carefully covered up. He was a threat to the continued security of Lee Carson.

"Come in," I said through stiff lips.

He went to the glass-and-bamboo bar and helped himself to a straight shot of bourbon. He didn't offer to pour me one.

"Okay, Jim Wirkus," I said. "Make it good, and make it fast. I don't have a lot of time."

He wiped his mouth. "That's right, you don't have a lot of time."

I flared at him. "Say what you mean!"

Wirkus poured another three inches into his glass, hooked a chunky elbow over the bar top. "You're cute, Miss Carson—damned cute. So tricky that it took me a month to find you. A month and three, four thousand miles. It's a long way from Miami."

That clicked. Miami, Frankie Fry—the man on the beach the same man standing in the parking lot and staring after Frankie's car as we drove off. I thought of the ready carbine again, of how it would be to slam a handful of bullets through this calmly dangerous man. Not here; I couldn't do it here. That would pose too many problems. I'd have to get rid of his body, for one thing. Somewhere else, then. The desert was a big and lonely place. A million corpses could be hidden in its faceless dunes.

"I don't know what you're talking about," I said.

"Didn't expect you to admit it," Wirkus sighed, and took his replenished drink over to the couch.

My mouth was dry. I spooned ice into a glass and covered it with liquor, drank half of it off, then stared cold-eyed at him. "You've got about one minute to make yourself clear, Mr. Wirkus—then I call the police."

"Two corrections there," he said. "Make that Lieutenant Wirkus, and don't kid me about the cops. They already know I'm in town. It's a kind of courtesy to check in with the locals, when you're a visiting cop."

A cop! My mind skidded. What the hell did a cop have to do with Frankie Fry? The angle came immediately to mind. Wirkus was on the take, being paid off by the ex-bookie.

He shook me with his next words. "This isn't a squeeze, Miss Carson. It isn't much of anything, really. I just thought I'd let you know you're not getting away with it forever."

"With w—what?" I asked, cursing myself for the tremble in my voice.

His pale eyes peered steadily at me. "Murder."

I forced a laugh. "I don't think you should finish that drink, Lieutenant. You must have taken aboard quite a load at Elva's place. Murder? Tell me, Lieutenant—do I look like a murderess?"

Jim Wirkus slowly shook his head. "No, you don't. Not if there's any kind of standard that applies. Generally, murderers look like anyone else. That goes for the female murderers, too.

But you look like a sweet, young girl. Only I know better, Miss Carson. Or should I call you Widow?"

I really flinched that time, but covered my involuntary start by downing the rest of my drink and putting the glass back up on the bar. My hands were steady as I lighted a cigarette. "I think this discussion is at an end," I said. "Anything else can be said through my attorneys."

His hard mouth lifted at the corners. "Oh, you're not under arrest. I'd have had to bring one of the locals with me, for that. I don't even have a warrant. In fact, I don't have much evidence. None that would stand up in court, anyway."

I felt better. "What do you have, Lieutenant?"

He spread his hands. The fingers were strong and stubby, with pale hairs curled on their backs. "A series of pretty good leads; strong hunches; whatever it is that makes a cop certain he's right; a few pieces of thin circumstantial evidence. As I said, Miss Carson—nothing that would hold up in court."

"Tell me," I said. "Since you've intruded on my privacy, you might as well try to be entertaining, at least."

He held out his glass. "I get dry, talking so much. You mind?"

"Oh, no; why should I mind? It isn't every evening an uninvited guest calls me a murderess."

Wirkus accepted the fresh drink I brought him. His fingers brushed min. They were warm. I wondered what the hell I was thinking about.

"I'll tell you what I've got," he said. "It all starts with a cute schoolgirl getting herself picked up on the beach. By a slob who went for schoolgirls in a big way. I always hoped to tag Frankie for a statutory, rape, or contributing to the delinquency of a minor. That's one of the reasons I was tailing him that day." "And?" I prompted.

"And I saw you drive off with Frankie. I saw the books he carried for you. A cop trains himself for the details. One book was on Anthropology, the other, Sociology. A couple of note-books, too."

I sipped at my own drink, my mind racing. Wirkus wanted something from me. Not money, he'd said. What then?

"The motel," he continued. "Frankie lost me before you got to his special cabin. Took me more than two hours to find the place. Never would have, if it hadn't been for Frankie's flashy car."

More than two hours, I thought. That meant Wirkus wasn't around when I pumped those two slugs into Frankie Fry. It meant I was gone when he did arrive. Wirkus didn't have a thing to go on. Ice rattled in my glass as I tried to understand how he knew so much, then—how he managed to trail me all the way out to Palm Springs.

"You know," he said, "Frankie should have been killed years ago. But not like that; legally, with his skinny neck stretched."

"Then why bother?" I said.

His mouth thinned. "Nobody's got the right to play God, Miss Carson. Besides there is no God—there's just men. And men should let each other alone. Nobody in this world is big enough to say this man dies and that man lives. Hoods, hustlers, con men—they've all got the same rights."

"And cops?" I said recklessly.

His eyes glittered. "And cops."

I started to have another drink, then thought better of it. I'd need a clear head to deal with this man. "You haven't explained how all this has anything to do with me."

His face didn't change. "You're in it, all right. I tried to close the town off when I found Frankie's body, sent men to train, and buss stations, to the airports. They had your description, right down to your bobbysox. After that, when nothing came in, I

140

figured you drove into Miami, and that you'd holed up somewhere. Now where would a smart killer pick? Not the exclusive
hotels; not the rundown joints, either. Both are too noticeable.
That left the middleclass motels. It took a lot of legwork to check
out all of them."

I shrugged. "This is all very interesting, but—"

"It'll get better," Wirkus promised. "A bookstore clerk
remembered the girl who'd bought some textbooks. Not many
calls for them in the summer, he said. Of course, the license number of the car showed on the motel's book, and the desk clerk's
description matched that of the guy in the bookstore."

"How clever," I said. "You traced the girl's car through its
license plate."

"No. The plates were phony. At least, the number sequence
was. But they couldn't be completely changed; the letters pointed
toward a certain county in Georgia. Atlanta's in that county."

I felt cold. The man was a bloodhound, an implacable tracker
who'd follow the tiniest lead to its conclusion. He was also one of
the rare breed, a dedicated, honest and stubborn cop. That made
him doubly dangerous.

Wirkus finished his drink. "I didn't expect to find the car in
Atlanta. But I had a place to start. I tried the airport first. And
what do you know, Widow? You're so sweet and pretty that the
ticket agent remembered you perfectly. Dorothy Dixon, you were
on the manifest. Funny how when somebody's picking a name,
they either make it euphonic or use their own first initials. L.C.
and D.C. aren't too far apart, are they?"

I grimaced. "Now you're a semantics expert."

"I know a little about a lot of things," Wirkus said. "I was
twenty-six hours behind you at Merid airport. Guess I should
have hurried more. But the stop wasn't wasted. The paper had a
story about the accidents down at Shuba."

I decided I'd have that drink, after all. And another cigarette. Anything to keep my hands busy.

"I came from a small town, too," Wirkus went on. "A place called Fort Pierce. It's bigger than Shuba, but not so big that folks didn't have the same talky habits. Everybody in Shuba was eager to chat about the Finneys dying like that—one by water, one by fire. The Finneys were real backwoods trash, they said. They didn't blame that girl for running off in the night like she did. They didn't even blame her for taking a couple of shots at Pete and Jett. No telling what they were trying to do to her, after her ma died."

Damn them, I thought. Sure, the storekeepers and land-owners and churchfolks would tsk-tsk and shake their heads over the Finneys and the half-grown girl out in the shack. But what the hell had they done about it? Just talk. The damned town lived to talk.

I went quickly across the room and flung open the door. I peeped out, shut it again, and went to each window in turn. Then I came to stand over him. "Mind standing up and opening your coat?"

He came up slowly, shaking his coat pocket, unbuttoning the jacket to show me the filled shoulder holster and nothing else. "No tape recorder," Wirkus said. "Nobody outside, either. I like to work alone, mostly."

"I'm not admitting a damned thing," I said. "I'll only say this: get the hell away from me, man. Get far away and get fast away."

"Or I'll get hit like Frankie Fry?" he said. "You're beautiful, baby, but you're more man than woman. Or maybe just poison-ous. But cold, baby—cold."

I shoved myself hard against him, crushing my breasts flat into his wide chest. I kissed him open-mouthed, searchingly, my arms coiled tight around him and my body writhing into his.

"There," I said, when I let him go. "Was that cold? Was that more man than woman? Now get out of here, cop. I'm tired of listening to your fairy tales. Run on back to your two-bit bootleggers and grubby cracker women, while I'm still feeling charitable."

"You wench!" he said, and backhanded me across the mouth.

I sat down hard, my skirt flying up around my hips, my legs sprawling. But I came up quick, spitting, raging.

"Oh no," I hissed, "Oh no!"

My head slammed into his belly. I tried to hammer a clenched fist into his crotch. Staggering back, Wirkus caught it on his bunched thigh. I went for his eyes then, clawing hooked fingernails. Blood spurted from his cheek, but I missed blinding him. A knee jarred into my stomach, a big hand clamped my wrists.

Savagely, I snaked my head forward and bit him deep in the corded column of his throat. A pain-filled noise whistled out of him, and he threw me violently from him. I crashed into the bar. A glass spun off the top and shattered on the rug. I pawed for an ashtray, flung it spinning at his head, and followed its flight in time to catch him ducking.

I kneed Wirkus in the face, chopped both hands down across the back of his neck as his head started to snap up. His clutching hands caught me around the waist as he fell forward, held tightly to me and dragged me down in a heap on top of him. His bent leg jammed itself between mine. I tried to squirm back, to get leverage so I could pound his face, so I could rip his eyes out.

I don't remember exactly when I stopped trying to maim Jim Wirkus. Everything got mixed up, rage boiling over into passion, hate fuming over into desire. I stopped trying to kill him, but I didn't stop fighting.

But then it was with other parts of my body. I battled with the aching mounds of my breasts, attacked with the timed striking of my hips, clenched and shook him with the muscled power of my legs. He was man; he was a threat; he was so damned sure of himself. This man really was sure of himself. And he'd called me cold.

I would show him. With the locked warmth of my mouth, I'd show him; with the writhing heat and smoothness of my body, I'd show him. No man could threaten me; no man could conquer me. I was a woman; I was sex incarnate, and I would be supreme.

I gripped his organ, squeezed it hard, thrust its throbbing head against my cleft, sucked his thing into me whether he wanted it that way or not. I slammed my vagina down over him, so that my pubic hairs mixed with his, so that our heat and sweat and dampness blended. He was big and bulky, but I took him in as if he was a child playing at being a man.

I rocked on him, twisted on him, flattened my breasts against his wide and hairy chest and bucked at his belly. I rolled over on top of him, straddled him, rode him like a damned back country mule until he spurted madly inside me in an orgasm he couldn't hold back.

The room whirled as he rolled me over, as he threw me down and held his thing crammed deeply into me. I struggled to get back on top, to dominate him, to make him come again and again until he was so damned weak he'd faint or pass out or do something else just as unmanly.

He wouldn't let me up. The son-of-a-bitch was raping me. He was the Finneys and the broad in prison and every other bastard who'd done things to me when I didn't want them to. I tried to bite him in the belly and he hit me in the mouth so that I tasted blood. He slammed that rod into me up and down and back and forth while I wriggled and tried to back off it, to slide off it. He fed it to me hard and strong and pounding, and I felt the goodness growing along my legs and bruised thighs and into my vagina where it exploded with a violence that shook my backgone.

I didn't quit. I fought him with blows of my pelvis and bites of my vulva, with the trained grasping of muscles within my vagina. I rolled and wiggled and hunched and stroked, trying to bring him to another orgasm and yet another. I'd drain the bastard, melt him, eat him up.

The battle raged through us, quivering, trembling, building to a massive, thundering explosion that shook the stars. But he didn't surrender, didn't turn away. I fought him again, determined to drain his strength, to prove where the power lay. And again the cresting, the might foaming of a runaway whirlpool. And again.

It was impossible. I refused to believe the weakness that was sapping the vitality of my loins, that was draining away the grip of my arms. I clawed at him; I lanced teeth into his shoulder; I used every bit of experience I had.

He beat me down. Damn him, he forced me into a broken, submissive hulk—into a passive, accepting woman. I must have been crying for some time. My cheeks were wet when he let me go at last. My mouth was dry. My body grew a thousand weary pains. Damn him, damn him.

I hid my face in my hands, choked back the sobs. It couldn't have happened. It just couldn't have happened. Not to me, Lee Carson. Not to The Widow.

His voice struck down at me. "Maybe this should have happened a long time ago, Lee. Maybe you would have been a real woman, if it had."

I said it through my fingers: "Don't feel sorry for me, you son-of-a-bitch."

He didn't answer, and I took my hands away from my flaming face. "A real woman? You mean a female you can use when you damned well want to, and only when you want. to. Is that what a real woman is? Something you can run on, and sell, and trade and beat? Is that being real?"

He bulked tall, standing up. "I almost wish—"

I sat up, snatched my skirt down. "You wish what? That I'd turn myself into something you can own? Don't make me spit, Wirkus. Don't make me throw up on my nice clean rug. You're no different than the rest. Let me open my legs and shake myself, and you're ready to call it love. Go to hell. Take your love with you."

"That wasn't what I meant," he said. "I almost wish I hadn't even seen you on that beach in Miami, that I didn't track you down, that I didn't know you're a cold and deadly killer-for-hire. No, I could never love you, Lee. I've spent my life hating your kind. But I might have loved you once—before you turned into what you are."

My lips were numb, tasting of betterness, of his sweat and blood. "Get out. You're just a lousy cop who had an itch for me. That's all you wanted, with all that talk about trailing me, about some imagined gun-girl. Get out, Jim Wirkus. Get the hell out of here and let me alone." But inside I knew different. This man, this self-sufficient man who was all man, had given me the truth I could never forget.

He turned at the door, this man who had conquered me, who had brought a thousand hidden, feminine emotions to the surface. "You're the one who'd better get out, Lee—if you have time. I said before that no man has the right to say who will die. I didn't stay with my own beliefs. When I knew I couldn't bring you into court, that you'd been too smart to leave anything behind, I played judge myself—judge and jury. And I sentenced you, Lee Carson. I sentenced you to execution."

"Wha—what do you mean?"

His head was down, his shoulders slumped. "You should be able to figure it out. I know about the Combine; all cops know about it. We don't laugh it off like the citizens do. Tracking you down, I left word here and there that I was looking for The Widow, that I had enough on her to send her to prison for live."

Any icy snake coiled itself slithering around my head. "But— that will bring them—"

"Yes," he said. "Your bosses won't want you around any more. They'll be afraid that you might make a deal to save yourself. They'll send some of your own kind after you, Lee. And I don't think you'll be able to avoid them. I didn't like doing it, Lee. But this world is in trouble. Sometimes violence is needed to right things."

He said something else as he went out of the door and closed it after him. It sounded like, "I'm sorry."

CHAPTER SEVENTEEN

T he lights are out downstairs. The house is very still, its brooding silence broken only by the noise of my typewriter. My white T-Bird is in the carport, but I'll never try to take it out of there. It's too easy to spot. I don't hear anything outside, but then, I wouldn't, no matter how hard I listen. They don't have to hurry. There's plenty of time.

I've been sitting in front of the typewriter for nearly two weeks, trying to get it all down in however much time I've got left, trying to tell how it was. I want to tell it. And maybe this story will keep some other mixed-up kid from going the easy way, too.

I'm not crying, this late in the game, and I'm not making excuses.

But I do have one regret. I wish it could have been worked out for me to be with a man like Jim Wirkus, before I picked up my first pistol. There's a real man, and I wouldn't have minded standing in his shadow and being a woman. I wonder—do all condemned women fall in love with their executioners?

No, I'm not going to put down a list of names and times and places. I'm not going to try and hide a little black book so the police can round up the Combine. In the first place, I wouldn't have much chance of getting away with it. My maids and gardener didn't show up for work more than a week back. They didn't send word why. They didn't have to. I know that somebody talked to them. The telephone? "Out of Order" long ago.

So I couldn't send any list out, if I wanted to. And I couldn't hide it in the house or around the grounds. They'll probably burn the house to be sure, and they've been waiting for me to come out for a long time now. They've got every door and window covered, day and night.

But they needn't worry. There haven't been many rules in my life, so I might as well stick to the few I've known. The major one is to keep my mouth shut. Call that a crazy criminal code, if you want; I don't care. It's the only code I've got. I knew damned well what I was getting into when I came into this game, and I'm not about to try and cry myself out of it.

I'm hungry. Just about all of my early life, I never had enough to eat at one time, and now here I am, hungry again. The refrigerator and cupboards ran dry three days ago. I've kept going on whiskey, but not too much of that, because I didn't dare pass out before I finished this, before I said everything I wanted to say.

The cigarettes ran out too, all except one that I've saved. It's here on the desk beside the manuscript. I'll light it, pretty soon, when I'm ready to go out.

I'm scared.

Just as frightened as when I was a sharecropper's kid back in Mississippi, when I was scared of everybody in the world. I'm not terrified of the guys waiting silently outside. I know what they are, and just what they'll do when I walk out of the door with that last smoke in my mouth.

But don't let anybody tell you they're not afraid of the grave. They'll be lying. I know.

I guess that's about it. I'll tie these pages together and drop them out of the bathroom window into the bushes. Maybe they'll get wet and last, if the guys outside decide to burn the house. Maybe somebody will get to read all about Lee Carson, The Widow.

It doesn't make a hell of a lot of difference, really. Lee Carson will be a long time dead by the time these words see print. If they ever do. But I guess I understand now what makes writers write. It's expressing yourself - whether anybody reads it or not. It's putting that wonderful, pure, all-important I into lasting form. This book is the only thing the real I has ever done. And it feels good.

I'm flicking an almost-dry lighter now. This cigarette tastes nice. I'm glad, because it has to last me the rest of my life.

All two minutes of it.

That's how long it'll take me to walk downstairs and out of the front door.

THE END